DEEP OVERSTOCK

#8: Structures

April 2020

❝ In limits, there is freedom. Creativity **❞** thrives within structure.

Edward Abbey

GARD - STRUCTURES

EDITORIAL

EDITOR-IN-CHIEF: Robert Eversmann

MANAGING EDITORS: Mickey Collins, Ariel Kusby & Z.B. Wagman

PROSE: Mickey Collins, Robert Eversmann & Z.B. Wagman

POETRY: Ariel Kusby

SOCIAL MEDIA: Ariel Kusby

COPYEDITORS: Ari Mathae, Caroline McCulloch, Elizabeth Neal & Kya Starling

INTERIOR DESIGN: Mickey Collins

COVER: Leanna Moxley

CONTACT: editors@deepoverstock.com
deepoverstock.com

Letter from the Editors

We first laid our foundation down with Space Exploration, just to try things out. Then we built it up issue by issue with Fairy Tales, Fables and Folktales, Paranormal Romance, Nautical Lore, Dreams, Westerns, Horror. Now we're here after two years and eight issues with Structures.

We had other options besides Structures, e.g. Novelty Cookbooks, Holiday Cookbooks, Production Bios, Country/Western Songbooks, Xeriscaping, Agriculture. But ultimately we decided on Gardening: Structures. Many of you asked, what on earth do you expect me to write? Am I to write blueprints for a jail? Or a how-to on a rocket launchpad? Designs for a raised rose bed? The gene sequence of a strawberry?

Yet, you have sent us—ingeniously—the architecture of an apple tree, living structures, pyramids, spaceships, skyscrapers, towers, wells, domes, even structures that strangle and stretch. Overall this is one well put together issue from start to finish, if we may say so ourselves.

So, what's next for Deep Overstock? We're going to put together a special issue: <u>New Arrivals</u>. For the first time Deep Overstock will be accepting work with no theme in mind. You can submit whatever never-before-published work you want!

We're looking forward to what you will write with the freedom of an open submission.

Yours,
Deep Overstock Editors

Chrysalis
by Amanda Depperschmidt

Each time I pass through the gate, I forget. I forget about the rusty nail, and it pricks my palm in the same spot, over and over: right hand, the bottom left mound of my palm, just above the wrist. The nail on the gate is rusted and twisted. Changing it would be a simple fix, were the problem not that I was always forgetting about it. Pass through the gate, descend upon the property, and suddenly it becomes difficult to remember anything at all. The soil here is rich and dark, and between a live oak tree and a small grove of palms sits a narrow but tall late Victorian home. The branches of the oak roll and intertwine as silhouettes against the side of the house, a shadowy flux upon the decaying red siding.

I have no memory of first arriving at this place and hardly a memory outside of it. A memory, like a house or a tree, should have a foundation, roots, a trunk. And yet for me there are only the idle days spent here, maintaining the home, exploring its rooms, and stopping for a snack in the garden. I am the property's personal preservationist. It is idyllic but difficult work, for between the cracks and the holes in the walls the house is spilling with moss, mold, and fungus which spread out and infect the framework. Just as Queen Victoria passed a blood mutation off to European royalty around the world, the houses built under her reign and in her name would come to suffer a similar kind of hemorrhaging.

Though I live within the property, I am not its owner. I am merely keeping up its appearance for my boss. The only reason she allows me away from the property is so that I may meet with her and report to her on how the house is doing. It is rare that she calls for me, though lately her invitations have become more frequent. The last time I saw her, I was invited to dine with her in the gardens of her corporate office. She had her attendant come, pick me up from the house, and take me straight to her building. She was sitting on a golden chair as her workers waved fronds above her head to keep her shaded. She is of a petite frame, but at times can seem like a giantess. Sprawled out at her feet, a naked body lay facedown on a log, and from the bare back she snacked on caviar, rare fish, and peeled mandarins.

"I would like to see that shabby dump turned into a beautiful garden, like the one Eve lived in before God sent her away," she said. Her eyes were black, always pitch black, and she always kept a smirk which hid any hint of discomfort or disagreement. Her attendant kneeled at her side and presented a turquoise box. She waved it open and pulled out two cigars, which she lit with a snap of her fingers and handed to me. "Now, tell me something interesting."

I bristled and her eyes narrowed in on me. I thought of something to say, but for a moment was sure I had told her once before. I hesitated, but spoke anyway against my better judgment: "Alles ist architektur. Everything is architecture. And everyone an architect."

She cackled. "So, you think yourself an architect? Or rather, a poet?"

"It is just a saying, ma'am. It means that everything is built up from something, and that everyone facilitates that growth." She took a puff from her cigar. "It's like the way the trees grow," I added, thinking of the shadows of the branches.

"Would you like to hear a saying that I know?" she asked. I nodded. Again she snapped her fingers and the trees behind her burst into flames. "Fire is blood, and blood is wood. Fire makes the blood rush, which turns humans into fine, hard wood." I blushed. "From you, I want only the finest wood." She laughed again. "And don't call me ma'am. Call me master."

That night I refused sleep, and spent the night instead carving arabesques into the crown molding of the home.

***

It is strange how memory works. How sometimes you can remember the ways of the world while forgetting your own experiences. I think about this while repairing squeaky faucets and scraping at bathroom tiles. Recollecting a feeling, preserved in a moment, causes a reaction within the gut. In the bathroom, mold covers the walls and the ceiling. I brush it, wash it, even occasionally find myself conversing and laughing with it. I have heard of others who stiffen at the sight of mold, stricken with fear at the mere form of it. It is as if the gut already knows all about the horrors of nature, the destiny of the body to be devoured and disintegrated, even if the brain is able to recognize it as momentarily harmless. The gut houses a second kind of memory.

The master's attendant waits outside for me; she has invited me to her private room. When I arrive she sits me down on her chaise and recounts a story from her past, the first she has ever shared with me. It is the story of how she was expelled from college after jealously setting fire to her younger sister's knitting club. She tells me how she angrily grabbed at the scissors, how her hair fell into her face, how she felt at that moment something else taking over her soul. There is no reason for her to tell me this. She excuses me as soon as her story is over, no explanation for why she shared it, no explanation as to why such an event would happen.

When I return home, the kitchen is on fire. I pull out a fire extinguisher from the closet, casting foam upon the flames until I can identify the source: a teapot, left boiling on the stove during my visit to the master's room. I open the windows and allow the smoke to dissipate. It takes three hours for the room to clear and the kitchen is left black, the appliances melted. The only thing that has survived the fire is the moss growing between the tiles on the floor.

I have read in a book from the house's library that when an untrained medium or a psychic leaves their mind open to spirits, occasionally an animal presence can take control over the mind in order to play tricks on humans. In the silence of the charred house I am able to give my thoughts to vessels—to the prophets, to Shiva, the god of destruction, riding on the faithful bull Nandi's back. Was I too just a pet to a destructive god? What could be the point to this job, of merely slowing the inevitable processes of decay? I leave the house and kneel in the garden, reaching my arms out in front of me to stretch the notches of my spine. I lie there for four hours until rain begins to pour down, and then I lie there for another two hours.

The next morning I have a recollection, my first memory. I remember being a kid and collecting caterpillars in an open terrarium for observation as they transformed into butterflies. I must have watched them for days or possibly weeks, but in one afternoon of inattentiveness, I left the terrarium outside and uncovered after going back inside to play. I forgot about the terrarium and left it outside and uncovered overnight, when it happened to rain. The next morning when I went out to check on the caterpillars, the terrarium had filled with water and the bodies of the caterpillars floated bloated in the brown water. The boy next door slapped me across the face at the sight of it, knocked me down, and kicked me in the stomach as I cried.

I do not know how to repair a burned kitchen. As far as I can remember, my job has only been one of conservancy. I have not been able to create or fix things anew, except for the occasional leaky faucet or hole in the ceiling. When there is no turnaround, no hope for salvation, it is the heart that loses out to anguish and apathy. I have no choice but to visit my master again in her room, my first time seeing her at my own behest.

I find her lounging on the chaise this time, puffing a cigarette and looking out her window at the buildings below. Buildings that she herself had designed and seen built, the landscape practically one of her own terraforming. I tell her what I have done and she says nothing, just allows me to weep in her lap. She strokes my hair with her cigarette hand, the ashes falling against the back of my neck.

"Would you like to hear another story?" she asks me, and I nod into her thigh. She tells me about the time she went big game hunting in the African savanna with a group of prominent investors and moguls. Wanting to impress them, she went after the biggest game she could fathom: a lion, proud and reclining, still growing into its long red mane. She stalked the lion all the way over to a large rock where it sprawled out in the sunlight. She watched it yawn, took a deep breath, and shot it right between its eyes. As she watched the blood trickle down its snout, she walked over to it, embraced it, and sobbed into its fur.

"Sometimes, things fall apart, rot, and die," she explained to me as if speaking to a child. "But if the lion had lived, I wouldn't have my favorite, warmest, and softest coat." The sun had set but neither of us got up to turn on a light. The master put the cigarette up to her lips for an inhale, but instead dropped her wrist down to the ashtray to extinguish the flame.

Returning that night I prick my finger on the gate as usual. The hole the nail has created in my palm is turning black with infection. Tetanus. I feel my throat close up. Once again I lie awake through the night. The bed on the second floor is canopied with mosquito netting, and as I toss on the mattress the net wraps up around me, tightening with each thrash. The scientific community once thought Chernobyl would be un-inhabitable for centuries. Now it is home to one of the most ecologically diverse populations on the planet. When creatures die at Chernobyl, there is no mold or fungi to break down their bodies. Instead their corpses are left perfectly intact, immaculately preserved. If I could stand up, on my tiptoes, I could brush the moss in the corners of the ceiling. There is no stopping it or holding it back. The mold is the owner of the house, and I am just a guest within it.

The next night the master again invites me back to her room, but I am too weak to meet her. I am forced to turn her down, and her attendant arrives to leave behind a gift: a preserved jungle ant, with a parasitic plant pushing out and blossoming from a crack in its skull. Its exoskeleton is covered in plant-like fur that has pushed through the shell of its body. It is beautiful; colorful; like a small fountain. I weakly bring it back to the library and place it on a coffee table. I am the ant; I understand why it was given to me. I open the small note attached at its base, which reads, "Don't call me your master. I am your owner." The ant and I are the gatekeepers, stuck between life and death, both caring for bodies neither of us actually own.

I spend the last day on my own in the library. I replay my only memory over and over in my head. The mold and the moss creep through the cracks in the walls like the caterpillars. They have all come out to watch. If I cannot keep the house preserved, how will its memories continue? What of my own memories, the memories of my owner? And who is keeping the memories of the Earth, while I am cleaning mold and repairing pipes?

I see colors and I believe it to be death. I see the wildness and the decomposers spread out and replace us on the land. I believe it to be death until she comes to me, not death, but my owner, to carry me out to the garden.

She lays me down against the brick foundation while she

waters the flowers. There are tears rolling down her cheeks and I ask her if she is crying because of me. She says no, she is not crying because of me, she is crying because of something that she remembered just then. This is the first time I see her in the house and she is beautiful here, and the house is perfect with her in it. The shadow branches arabesque down her back and arms like tattoos. Empty and abandoned cicada shells cling to the stone ornaments and tree trunks. I watch her noticing something, and she sets her watering can down and kneels to be closer to the ground. She brings her palm down to the dirt and allows a small garden snake to twist around her wrist. She cooes at it, strokes it, and winds it around her as I feel my own spine coiling.

I am having a dream where all the continents are twisted around my owner's wrists. In the ocean everyone is standing on each other's shoulders. Everyone is there and we are all building a tower. I am the last one left. The tower is stretching into the heavens. I climb up the backs of everyone, their faces laughing and familiar. When I reach the top, I sit atop the second-to-last person's shoulders. I reach my hands up to the sky and feel hands and wrists, streaked with soot, reaching back for me. I laugh because we have done it at last. We have rebuilt the spine.

Fifteen Eighteen AD

by John Chrostek

On the mustering grounds
of Argentoratum, where the Serments
de Strasbourg found its accord,
and hordes of hollow serfs wrought castle stone from tender
valley-grass,
upon that memory of masters, men and order,
the dance of St. Vitus came first upon
the lady Troffea and peeled open
the gatemouths of Hell.

It appeared at first like a compulsory fire.
The power of dance is of the blood,
the liquid heat of the philosopher,
the succor and flow,
the primal speak, the body-self, the beast.
At night, when gods have left us, it is a guide,
leading us into the coppice, the ever-dark and free.
Guided by that fire, Troffea
wove herself into a new reality
and rejected the Gifts of the Masters:
that which was *sacrum* and sane.

On the mustering grounds
one dancer became many
as evening paled to night,
as crow-songs bubbled
like shears. No one heard the joiners
consent or debate to dancing, no instrument
or melody spurred on the totentanz.
Words were already but wind.

Around the unending festival
of madness, architects of industry
toiled to compile forms and functions
in which to shape the pandemonium,
a fitting frame and stage to attempt a narrative control
and bring the people back from their deliria.
They thought to pin a meaning

to the spreading condition,
to the horror of its endurance, but meaning means
nothing to the divinity of skin.

The dancing carried on,
oblivious to the god-hand machine.
The dancers dropped, the curtain fell,
faces bent forever towards glee.

In time, the fire settled into wild grass
sprouting in the cracks of the floorboards.
The bodies were collected in a pit,
vacant sinews twitching
in the memory of a jig,
and the business
of the masters resumed,
haunted from the rafters
by the madness in its breaking,
as it best prefers itself to be.

Tetris®

by Sabrina Stein

It starts with the flick of a switch. The belt twitches on. An incessant, low hum fills the silence. But there never was silence, really. Just the noise of before, impossibly and beautifully peaceful in contrast to this reawakened monotony, this auditory hell. A bizarre rage stirs in the whir of eternity.

I am a grocery store bagger. I stand at the butt of consumerism. The anus, squeezing out its excrement in an agonizingly slow, oddly colored, bumbling assortment of shit. *"Successful bagging starts with a solid structure"* I recall sardonically in the serious tone of my grocery store supervisor as another bony bundle of celery writhes down the conveyor belt toward my withering gaze. With violent pleasure, I plunge the dripping stalks into a hole between the box of Yum Nut granola and vegan hot dogs. I smile under dead eyes, holding the bulging bag out to its bewildered owner. "Have a nice day."

The high of Tetris® is sweet; it satisfies. When I fill a bag perfectly, poetry dripping from my tired hands, I quell the urge to bow. The beauty of packaged food, collaged into prismatic frames, purchased by an ever-changing face is altogether astonishing. I hate my job, though, and excuse me if my mind wanders to the perverse; this happens within the first seven minutes of any grocery store bagger's shift.

Another transaction starts. The cashier amiably chirps at the poor cattle on the other side of the counter as they waddle through the chute. Their conversation is blissfully erased by the *beep beep BEEP* of items sprinting over the scanner pad. This cashier has fast hands, despite their slow lilt. I wait alone at the end of the check stand, marooned on an island of unnecessary labor. Just me and the incessant, humming belt. Nobody looks at me, nobody likes to talk to me. I hate everyone.

Bananas. They jerk grotesquely onto the counter space, squeaking to a halt in their rubbery skins. I push them to the side. Next come several bags of avocados (*these people are spenders*), apples, "organic" carrots with the whole plant still attached, butter, spaghetti jars, hummus, taco shells, French bread, wheat bread, more bread (*SEPARATE THE BREAD TO THE SIDE SO IT DOESN'T GET SQUISHED BY THE—*), thirty rack of cheap beer (*nod of approval*), chips, pretzels, multivitamins (*scam*), gum, potatoes, kiwis, sausage, raw chicken (*gross*). I pause mid-bag to walk around the counter for some hand-sanitizer.

Meanwhile the slew of fodder continues pulsating down the belt, roiling and pushing over itself. A huge box of cat litter barrels down the center, mowing everything out of its path… BUT WAIT, THERE IS A BLOCKAGE! And now the cat litter is frittering back and forth on the belt in some ecstatic masturbation against the black rubber before I take an arm and wipe a whole section of food out of the way so that the box finally releases and swoons down the rest of the belt into my waiting arms. A kiwi rolls over to the side, afraid. I am at once disgusted and moved.

"This job does not define me. My thoughts do not define me" says the note scribbled and taped above my desk at home. A life-long suppression of darkness does not allow dark thoughts, so they squeak out of air bubbled corners, pressing against my bedroom door at night, riding the infinite grocery belt like a sideways carousel. But what vulgar musings lie on the underside of that looping rubber? Plunging cucumbers, gouged tomatoes, strewn clamshells, torn chia seeds, impaled toothpicks, slathered oil…the list twists dark under and over in endless turns, primed with the flick of a switch. Let me bag that for you! Don't act surprised when I do a good job.

The Factory

by Bob Selcrosse

There are two factories on separate hills.
The hills enclose a little village.
The people live in tall grass. They live in huts made of grass.
Their children play in the grass.
The grass waves and the factories watch it.

Factory representatives drift through the grass—*our product is very good, very very good.*
Some children are drawn in like crickets. The company executives take the children in their arms and fill their mouths with grass. This is how the parents see them. They offer their blessing, as company executives are their source of bread and butter.

Some children become addicted and disappear into the grass.
Once a year, near Christmas, parents are retired and children are reaped.
Some mothers hide children, as if they weren't born.
The old wander the grass. They hunch as if their backs were beach balls.

The old lie low and tempt the children.

Children, among their many missions at war, bump into the old.
Read a goddamn book! they say before perishing.
The old are thin like paper. In a fire, they raise into the sky.

Books are not made of grass.

The people attempted to block out the factories with chimney smoke. The factories took their wood away. Representatives knocked on every door, came in, stamped out each fire in big black boots. Light is illegal.

The factories began making ash.
Ash cacked from the smoke. Ash cacked from the chimneys.
Ash cacked from the babies who, clutched by their fathers, could not blink anymore.

Finally, now that the sky was ash and the ash was sky, the people could live.
Company executives could not peer through the ash as they could through the grass.
The families, in their privacy, forked their plates full of grass. Ash, ash. It tasted of ash!

No title
by Sarah Wei

what is the cost of a beating Heart?

what numerical value to it
can we assign?

and whose is its
to mine?

to claim
takes but a Second

a Lifetime
some
to lose

20 *Planter's Box - Mark Hurtubise*

The Harrowing Tale of Wyoming Jack-Rabbits

by Dan A. Cardoza

I can't get enough interstate I-80, between Melissa and her recent past. I never anticipated that I'd see so many dead jack-rabbits.

Tommy isn't far behind. I'm convinced of that. I know Tommy very well. I'm his brother from another father and his best friend. My older brother Tommy is the one who defended me in high school, kicked the shit out of a few of my bullies. The Tommy I know is good-natured, with a Big Sky heart.

In college, we shared a friendly competition. This included who made the most touchdowns and who ran 400 meters the fastest. I'll be honest here. Tommy always seemed to have the edge. But, when it came to winning over the girls, I'd say it's a dead heat.

We both graduated honors, Tommy, Agriculture U.C. Davis, 25 touchdowns over his college career. I went down south, San Diego State University, an M.S. degree in Bioengineering, 23 touchdowns. Not bad for two boys from Wyoming.

~~~

Tommy laughed at the restraining order, said, "If I can't have you the devil can."

It's not long before we've crossed Salt Lake City, Utah, and then up into the mountains toward Western Wyoming.

"Levi, the sky is endless here."

Before I answer Melissa, there's another thumb. A thwack! "I know," I say and look in the rearview, "I haven't driven this highway for years."

Directly in front of me, is 240 miles of freeway that stretches clear to the city limits of Cheyenne, Wyoming. They're a lot of things I want to keep in the past, but I can never forget the damned Wyoming jack-rabbits.
~~~

I say to myself that Tommy is far behind us, but deep inside, my instincts tell me that's not true. I bet he feels like he's traveling into the past, so far away from his long term comfortable home, in the hills near the Ghost Mill. Ghost Mill is what we call the long-abandoned lumber town of Tennant, California. Tennant's sawmill, company store and housing, has been abandoned and emptied of people and trees since way back in the Twentieth Century. Wealthy Northeast industrialists made sure of that, with their insatiable appetite for timber and pulp-money. These days, at least in Siskiyou County, the Fed's won't let you snap a matchstick, unless you can prove its flame is sustainable. So, who needs another lumber mill, right?

The good folks of Wyoming joke that they're more jack-rabbits than humans in their fine state. Equal Rights is their state motto.

~~~

"I'm only human," said Tommy. This was his standard, counterfeit apology for giving Melissa another bloody lip. It was difficult for him to think he'd made mistakes until the thought of losing her again. But this time, there was no turning back.

As a small child, Tommy's father beat our mother worse than the family birddog, just because he wouldn't chase quail. This all happened, before I was born. Now Tommy barters his father's abuse for sympathy, and uses it as an excuse for every shortcoming and failure in his life. His attitude is the very least of his deficiencies. He is both masochistic and sadistic, a rare diagnostic amalgam. He gets high from his emotional pain when he hurts someone. What I've come to learn, these past several months is that deep down inside, he knows that he and his dead father are evil as fuck.

Maybe there is such a thing as Karma, and things do come back to haunt you, or maybe take sweet revenge. But Melissa wasn't going to stick around to find out by running out the clock.

I can remember when Tommy was a teenager, maybe his freshman year of high school. Tommy's biological father had been dead going on two years by then, but he still reached out from his grave. His father was T-boned and died in the middle of an intersection. Upon hearing this, Tommy expressed very
~~~

little emotion. Upon his demise, there wasn't a will. The only thing he left Tommy was a legacy of rage, and anger, gifts that keep on giving.

Tommy kept everything in a knot in his stomach, somewhere deep inside, an incubator for angst and tumult. He complained of a bellyache 24/7. I recall sitting in the family room with him, watching T.V. He'd keep one of the sofa pillows tight over his abdomen. He said it helped him relax and even joked once, "It's one of the ways you can hold everything bad inside you. Know what I mean Levi? It's like the horror movie, Alien Resurrection, when they discover most of the cargo on board are mutated humans on life support, all part of a grand experiment."

Mother said Tommy's behavior was just a nervous habit, not part of any larger psychological symptom, something he'd outgrow. Sure her husband used to beat him, used a belt or a strap that she provided. She couldn't tell you why she bawled in the other room. His father's excuse was that Tommy was no good at making decisions. And, that the ones he made were disasters. Mother wasn't sympathetic, never had a problem with any of his discipline.

She was part of the conspiracy. She never raised an eyebrow when he called Tommy "a goddamned sissy and worthless," as well as other horrible names that leave deep emotion cuts that even time refuses to heal. His father said Tommy needed "a little redirection."

But as bad as he was, there were many days Tommy missed his dad.

~~~

Not long after leaving Salt Lake City, we find ourselves ten minutes east of Rock Springs, on the pie crust edge of the Wyoming plains, some 259 miles from Cheyenne. Dodging tumbleweed and bucking headwinds, I keep my eyes in the rearview in case his blue Tesla X shows up. Melissa is in the back seat now, crunched into a ball. She's sitting with her knees against her chin, and her bare feet on the seat. She's pensive as hell and afraid for her life.

Tommy isn't a renaissance man. He'd tell Melissa, "If you
~~~

need one of those, try New York City, in the Off-Broadway district or the Castro, in 'Frisco." He doesn't know what the hell an Untuckit is, doesn't damned care. He's all about his blue jeans and long sleeve denim, and the outdoors.

Tommy's the type of husband that only says, "I'm sorry," if there's something in it for him. He's not apologetic for how he thinks a man should behave. He's a chiseled shaving off his ole man's wooden block. He's plenty smart. He just doesn't show it. There's a blind spot in his head, the size of the Titanic. It's only a matter of time before he's going down.

~~~

In short order, we whisk through most of Wyoming. We're now twenty minutes shy of the city limits of Elk Mountain. Across the state, I count dead rabbits. Since I've had lots of time on my hands, I've concluded that the jack-rabbits in Wyoming have H.D.H.D. Don't quote me, but I think they'd be less likely to get run down and messed up if they just chilled. They're too damned hyper, too quick to bullet in any direction, every-which-away. And, they always seem to find a way to run right under your tire. But I give them credit. They're smart sunsza-bitches, very good at match.

At least the jack-rabbits in Wyoming are. On the I-80, you don't have to lower your head to look at the odometer to check your mileage. You only need to count the dead rabbits up ahead. Tommy and I have done it so often, going back and forth to college. Dead rabbits are better than any odometer. Each dead Fur-Frisbee is a designated mile. Do you get where I'm going here?

A jack-rabbit's understanding of calculus is unparalleled. When you see the first jack-rabbit, your odometer is registered at 20 miles. This is your starting point. So, for each dead rabbit, you've used a gallon of gas. And so, when you count your rabbits, when you've counted 15, you've traveled 300 miles. So you don't need an orange, low gas warning on your dashboard to get you excited. At 15 of those furry bastards, just find the nearest gas station and fill up.

And be sure to stay alert. If you are unfortunate enough to hit one of the skinny ones, hungry, and dressed in bones, you might get a jagged femur in your tire.
~~~

~~~

It's a little complicated, so I will attempt to unmuddy things. Melissa is Tommy's second wife, my first. He borrowed her to fill his need for a bookkeeper. It wasn't long after she began her new job, he stole her from me for good, with his charm and bravado. She was at a vulnerable place in her life. We needed the money. It wasn't long before Melissa was Tommy's new wife at the BigT Cattle Ranch.

The ranch is located just outside of Sierraville, California. Part of me still thinks Tommy knew exactly what he was doing. I learned a quick lesson here: never give a pyromaniac matches.

I should've known better. He is a lucky S.O.B. with his dangerous blue eyes, chiseled good looks, and the cattle ranch, let alone all his bank accounts.

It wasn't long after that Melissa and I amicably divorced. I was the best man. Now my best friend had him a personal bookkeeper and my ex-wife. I couldn't help but imagine those two together, really cooking the books.

Once all the testosterone and estrogen settled down, I was truly happy that they found one another. After all, Tommy was my friend, and Melissa was my forever love.

Since then, we've remained close friends over the years. Sometimes good people just make honest mistakes and move on. That is why God made erasers. We all learned to forgive each other that way.

~~~

As we near the city limits of my early childhood, in Cheyenne, I feel unsettled. Melissa and I can't wait for another chance, though I have a hunch, it will take place apart more than together. All the running we are doing is for her sake.

Before we drove off into new futures, before we could find a safe place for Melissa, she told me some of the things Tommy would say to her.

"Your lipstick is too red for a lunch date with an old girlfriend. An extra night in Reno, at the convention, is too much."

She'd ask Tommy, "Is this is how it all starts, the abuse, like a leaky faucet before it turns into a waterfall, and carries you over the top? When can I stop lying about all the bruises here and there, from bumping the corners of cabinets or the edges of cupboard door?"

When we'd occasionally meet for coffee, she'd wear her sexy sunglasses, indoors.

I felt helpless. All I could do at first was listen, hopefully provide comfort.

"You can't fly out to California," he'd say.

"But, it doesn't look like mom has much time left."

His back talk, "Then Melissa, there's one more reason not to go."

Questions became requests that morphed into pleading. Tommy's answers grew relentless. Every damned one was no.

"No, you don't need to see a doctor. I'm sure it's only a few cracked ribs," he'd say. "No, I don't give a shit how dry the snow-pack is in Park City, Utah. You can ski right here up at Donner, or North Star."

"Hell no," he'd say. "You don't need to attend your fifteen-year class reunion."

Melissa said it wasn't long before she felt like a cheap bar code on the side of a bottle of hydrogen peroxide. Too soon, she'd struggle to remember the names of her nieces and nephews. She hadn't seen them since she could remember.

She'd shut the drapes when the sun and the sky were beautiful outdoors. It didn't take long before she started looking for a way out. Anywhere else, a safe space, even death, began looking like shelter.

~~~

We thought we might outsmart Tommy. Keep him looking for us in Cheyenne for a while, where he predicted we would be. After all, in Cheyenne was our home, where all families' psychological bodies are buried. Cheyenne is where we are
~~~

from.

It hasn't even been 24 hours yet. We've been driving non-stop. I'm using the odometer again. I ran out of rabbits. We haven't seen many in the contoured mountain roads of North Carolina. They seem to know how to bend left and right here, just when you don't expect them to.

It's possible jack-rabbits are smarter here in the Blue Ridge Mountains. The direction we're heading is in front of us, somewhere still unknown, somewhere after tomorrow.

Melissa is now buckled up, on her side, asleep in the backseat. Usually, that's Cherry's spot, my golden retriever. I removed Cherry's blanket I keep on the Highlander's leather seats. There won't be any duck hunting for a while, no mud. Melissa is wrapped up in my black leather coat. It's so quiet now. I can hear each twitch, each moan. It's like I remember Cherry, when she's was asleep, at my feet, in front of the fire.

I can tell the way Mellissa moves her feet that she's running in her dreams. What I don't know is where she is going. With my Cherry, I always assumed she was chasing a mail carrier, or snapping at someone's speeding tire speeding down the street.

~~~

It's late Thursday when we pull in front of the Holiday Inn in Asheville. But not too late, they still have rooms. After two flights of stairs, I carry Melissa across the threshold like I did when we eloped. I get us twin beds and a good T.V. with lots of porn.

It's not long before she's fearful again. So afraid, I sit on the dirty carpet in front of the bathroom door while she takes a shower. Only after I tuck her in one of the beds, do I turn on the television. Nothing is exciting, not even late-night television sex, so I leave it on, and turn down the volume on the Weather Channel. Melissa finally makes soft noises. She's beginning to drift out into the deeper waters of sleep.

I'm exhausted too, but vigilant. It's about one in the morning now, when I noticed her cell phone light up and vibrate next to her bed on the nightstand. I snatch it up to quiet it down,
~~~

stop it from shaking. Her cell is on vibration mode. Even under the covers, I can see that she's shaking and shivering again.

I slowly read the text. It's from Tommy. It's from his work phone, back home. It says he's in the parking lot and on his way up. I take the blanket from my bed and place it over Melissa until she stills again.

~~~

I worked my way through college, driving electrical parts all over Sacramento, California. My future father-in-law gave me my first real job. It was either that or back home for the summer to buck alfalfa hay in wired up bundles for three months.

Dick and I would, on occasion, share long philosophical conversations. Though we would one day be related, if only by marriage, I considered him more of a friend. One time, over a Coors or two, Dick explained that if you live your whole life with only a handful of friends, you will be a fortunate man. He held up his palm and showed me four fingers and a thumb. After he died, there was only Tommy. I had one friend left.

~~~

When I pull the drapes apart, they're stiff and smoky. Outside it's misty, and the parking lot is as shiny as tar. The mask of humidity in the air looks ominous and heavy for this time of year.

Someone is walking toward us now. I can barely hear the footfalls coming down the long, second story corridor. The steps soften, tiger paws before a kill.

I glance at the muted Weather Channel. There's a hurricane coming. I use the remote. It's the new Xfinity handheld, the one with a handgrip. Inside the room, there is nothing but blackness, like something's ending.

It's then I turn into a black panther. I become invisible. I relax in the extra hotel chair, sit on my haunches, and wait. I've placed my leather jacket on my lap. From inside the jacket's long, deep pocket, I pull out my .40 caliber Beretta. I glance over at Melissa. I can't help but believe she's dreaming of a brand new life. Her lovely face is pulsing in the red wash of the cheap hotel digital alarm clock. This is the alarm clock, in every damned hotel, in America, that is always set, precisely at the wrong time.

Tommy won't have to knock twice to enter. I've left the door unlocked. Unfortunately, this is going to wake up Melissa.

Tales of Old Soldier
by Ben Crowley

The Bridge
Old Soldier comes to the bridge. It is broken.
Men pick up stones to fight.
Old Soldier remakes the bridge, shouting at them.
He throws stones into the water until the water is dammed and
they can cross to fight him.
He shouts at them to kill him if they dare.
He shouts at them to throw stones.
He shouts and they throw stones and he continues to build the
dam.

The Bath
I have a thick white granite hole into which I ladle blood, says
Old Soldier.
The blood ferments within a week. It is a lusty drink.
When the blood runs down the hill and collects into the bath,
Old Soldier stands as still as time. He believes in the blood.
I am the original man.
The original man.

The Cave
Old Soldier removes his armor.
He takes it to the Forbidden Realm, the humming womb.
I'll protect no one! No! Not ever again!
Old Soldier bundles the armor.
Old Soldier cannot be an island unto himself, says Old Soldier.
Old Soldier hurls his armor inside.

The Keep
Old Soldier must have the wind and the rocks.
The wind went away. Then the rocks went away.
My progeny is too vast, Old Soldier laments.
Some of them terrible.
Old Soldier kneels atop the mountain and shoots every bird
from the sky.
There are still some circling. If only Old Soldier were a little
higher.
He climbs the trees and in the highest one stands at the very

top.
Now he shoots the highest birds.
Dead, they have covered the mountain.

The Mound
Old Soldier hears a ticking heart.
The heart of one remaining bird.
He can hear it in the faces of the cliffs.
He can hear it from the hollows of the trees.
He buries the bird under a mound of rocks.
He builds the mound three times as high as Old Soldier.
Old Soldier, under the attack of life, prays to the sun.
The sun will not blink. Old Soldier will not blink.
The sun has neither eyes nor conscience.

The Crevice
Old Soldier has put all fingers inside every crevice of this
mountain.
Until there was a crevice like the bone of a whale.
Old Soldier ran his hands up and down it.
It is like a bow left behind by a giant.
One end goes up toward the sun. One end goes up near the
moon.
There is no way Old Soldier could wield it.
But he can feel it, and he is grateful.

The House
The sign of the house says "Old Soldier."
Old Soldier may not enter the house. The house is locked.
The house is full of swords.
That's Rusted Blood he sees through the window. With him I
slew the Georgic army.
And there that's King's Bane, with him I slew the King of
France.
There were more swords, all of which might have belonged to
Old Soldier.
But Old Soldier had been alive too long and could not remem-
ber.

The Tent
Old Soldier sits in the door of his tent.
Old Soldier asks the stars for one last breath.
Old Soldier holds that breath for a hundred years.

Structures That Strangle & Stretch

by S. C. Downey

Deconstructing patterns and stories is hard as hell…
the hell we create by needing to be right.

The way we fight to defend that which we believe…
believe to be real and true about the world.

We cling desperately to a story…
any story that makes us feel less alone.

We reach for the nearest branch…
in order not to drown in uncertainty.

The longer we cling…
the longer we stay stuck.

Life is supported by a powerful current…
a current that will carry us where we need to go to arrive home.

It takes courage to let go, to trust…
to reach before knowing what will keep us afloat.

Those who endure and enjoy the journey…
build strong rafts from gratitude, love, faith, friends and family.

Our lifeline is weakened…
by indifference, righteousness, judgment, cruelty and hate.

We do have a choice…
and may not find ourselves alone, clambering when the branch
breaks.

Reach bravely for that which you care about most…
trust and know you are safe.

Never give up on what is deeply real…
be curious and dance with wonder.

Every bug, leaf and bog is filled with extraordinary complexity…
and you are no exception.

You belong and you are valued beyond measure…
by a magnitude that stretches from a single cell to an ever-expanding universe.

Hold on, let go…
and reconstruct from the inside out.

Everything you need is within…
without a doubt.

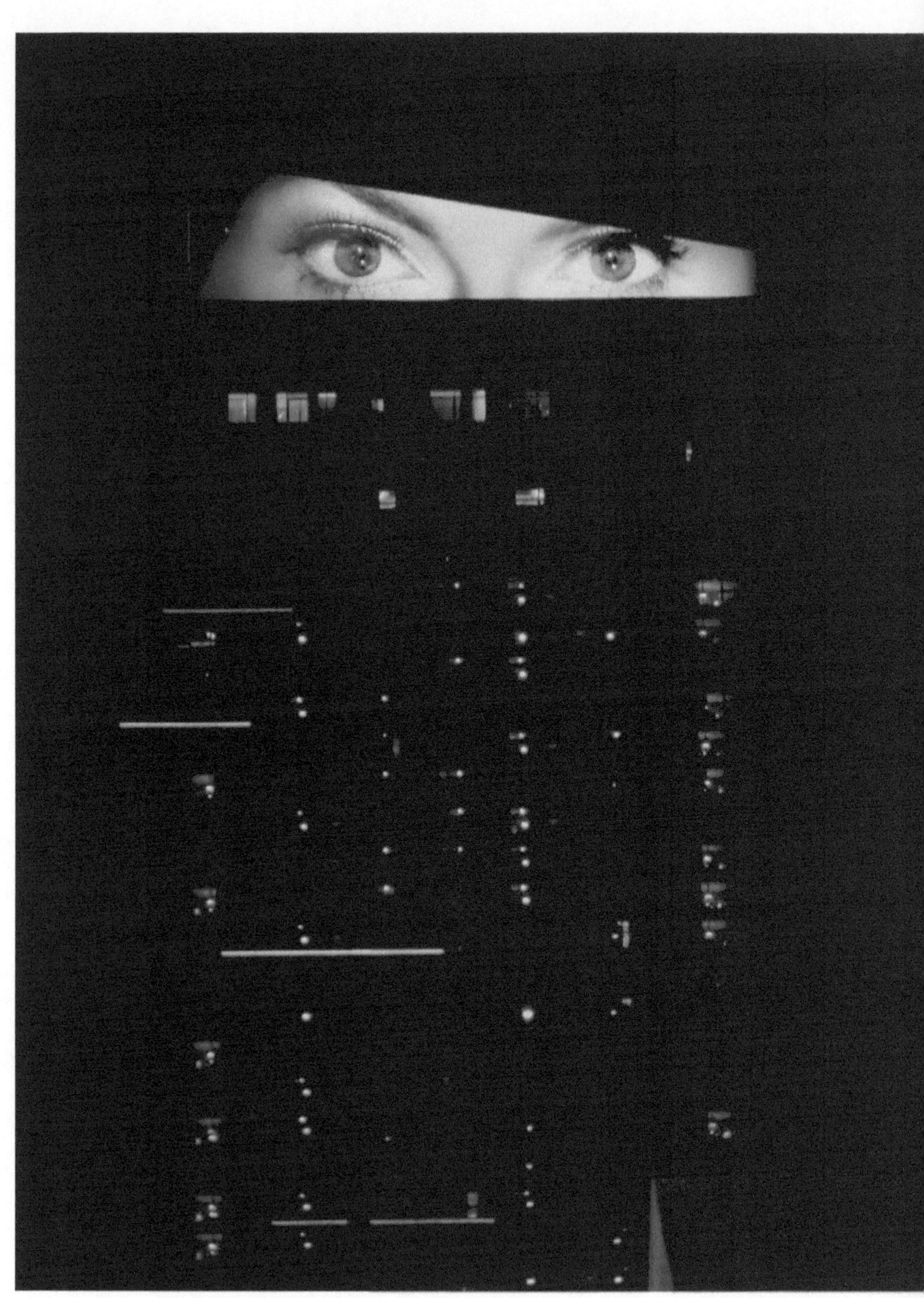

 Voyeur - Mark Hurtubise

The Vocation that has Chosen Me

by Holly Day

There will never be enough time to catalog
all of the dreams of the things in my yard
in my house: the fat squirrels that roost in the trees outside
the sparrows that peck at the dead insects in the air conditioner
set in the window
the mice that live behind my stove, the spider curled in wait
in the corner of my room.

They whisper their stories in Morse code raps
clicking mandibles and tiny, clawed feet, demanding
I stay up just one more hour, one more hour to trap
their thoughts with my pen, in words I can remember.

When I dream, it's of dust mites and fleas
bits of cheese left out on the counter, the warmth
of the summer sun, an explosion of flowers
the songs of the stars and a terror
of vacuums. There will never be enough time

to transcribe my cat's demands, the hopes and dreams
of the blind voles in my basement
all of these things I need to write.

Coterminous

by Hayden Moore

'In the elder days of Art,
Builders wrought with greatest care
Each minute and unseen part;
For the Gods see everywhere.'
(Longfellow)

Every morning, when the withered gray fingers of dawn cast a pale light in her room, Borea blew out of bed to see what time it was. Confusion was a masterpiece of the mornings. As she rubbed her eyes she fogged the window with her breath, Borea knew it could be anytime in the world. Sometimes it was a certain fashion of the people passing by. Perhaps it would be the population density or lack of motor vehicles. Bare-headed men and women betrayed a time after 1950. Some mornings revealed nothing but the trees and the river. A passing deer or hare reminded Borea that time was relative and the animal kingdom thought nothing of it. All that mattered to the hare or the deer was the illusion of Now. As she wiped the fog from the window, Borea looked again and saw. Her eager jaw dropped and she ran downstairs.

Just before she reached the door, Borea laughed at her bare feet. Had her mother been there, she would have scolded her. But the elements, no matter the weather, had no effect on the boundless curiosity of Borea. Just a turn of the knob and the door that shielded her from the world would submit. She counted to three and the doorknob squeaked a C-sharp before the sheer force of Borea's eager left-hand thrust open the ancient oak door. When the wind failed to blow, her dark eyes matched her dark gaping mouth as her red hair remained unmoved.

The pavement of the sidewalk was as smooth as polished marble and as pure as ivory in hue. Cars hovered by in perfect order in spite of their numbers. People passed by Borea like water does a rock jutting out of a stream.

"Rocks look like jewels in the waters passing through," she muttered to herself.

A pair of men of identical height, suits and hair glared at her as they passed. Borea touched her own face to make sure she was awake. She felt herself and nodded. It was then that she looked at the people on both sides of the street, in the passing cars without drivers or wheels. All were fair haired, all were blue-eyed, all were quite tall and all were silent as they marched in their respective directions. Even the trees lining the immaculate streets were pruned to perfection while the coffee shop just across the street promised: *The Purest and Perfect Cup Every Time*. Times past had always provided hilarity with the promise: *Best Coffee in New York*. Somehow, the promise across the street seemed valid and sent chills up Borea's spine.

Across Time, Borea had experienced a series of troubles. She had been called a whore, a witch, a hippie, a cunt, a devil, a stupid little girl, a goddess, a savior and nothing of much consequence in the better times. But this was the first time she felt that Time was out of joint. Borea felt drunk as she walked north amidst the marching multitudes in a well-groomed city with fluorescent lighting from the overcast sky. As she walked along the river, she noticed The Hudson had been straightened and the water was translucent. The faint smell of chlorine lingered in the windless air. Airships resembling zephyrs but octagonal hovered over the city. All bore the high-resolution image of some old blonde-man's wizened face with a smile and furrowed brows. It was then that Borea noticed the sky.

In the best of times, the city had been on the unsatisfactory side of air-quality. But nothing vast entered the life of mortals without a curse. Now, as Borea looked deeper into the firmament, she realized it was not cloud cover that cast the etiolated light on the city. It was a dome of some sort, an overarching wall covering the five boroughs. She suddenly felt claustrophobic for the first time in her life. Here she was, just another player in the game deemed good at some point, a game played by every one and excluded all the rest. Whatever it was that deemed a person fit to participate was abominable, Borea felt it in her bones. If she was a part of it, she was the only one without fair hair, flawless skin and gleaming blue eyes.

"Mongrel bitch," a girl her age said, with perfect articulation as she passed by.

"The one are many and the many are One without you," a

precocious toddler giggled, as he scurried by with his parents.

"The ape which apes find most beautiful still looks apish to non-apes," a middle-aged woman whispered, with excellent stage projection.

Like breath into the wind, Borea passed the passersby but heard every word spoken with clarity. By the time she had reached what used to be The Little Red Lighthouse—now painted a gleaming ivory—she sat by the crystal waters of The Hudson. What should have been New Jersey across the water, was nothing but a void. The George Washington Bridge was now a petrified monument to some cause leading nowhere. Borea watched as a flock of geese flew west into the void and vanished. Borea wept for the absence of everything that used to make the world messy. She touched her imperfect face and looked at the freckles on her shoulders that led down to her arms and diminished like a cluster of galaxies at her wrists. Her manic hair found no animation in the windless city. Every breath was Stygian. Borea shook her head violently and stood up. A shudder within told her to look up and she did.

Bones were what made the bridge to nowhere. Skulls acted as screws while femurs bore the greatest burden of the structure. The more delicate bones of the hands and feet adorned the suspension cables of cured sinew wound together like abominable cables of silk. Millions upon millions of pieces of people constituted the bridge to nowhere that nobody used. A red, white and blue flag with a single white star where fifty once were flapped in the artificial wind provided by some hidden machine. A single red stripe cut across the white square like a river of blood as perfectly aligned as The Hudson. Borea squinted her keen eyes and read a sign hanging on the bridge: *Construction Underway for The People - Date of Completion Immanent.*

Time had reached its terminus. All that remained was festering in its own immanence. Borea had experienced limits to space but never Time. Time moved mountains, it birthed universes, it ate its own children, it was the relativity never to be grasped but always experienced. But Time had leaked out of the world and this place remained. For the first time in her existence, Borea felt like she could never go back. If there was no going forward, back would no longer be back since it was the only direction to go. The whirligig of Time had brought back its revenge on itself. The Cosmic Serpent had eaten its own tail at last. Borea shook her head again to rid herself of the metaphors that seemed to make Time thinkable.

She felt the chlorinated air fill her lungs but she did not falter. Her vision sharpened and her skin tingled as her bare feet left the manicured grass, her left big toe lingering a bit as it always did. The People who witnessed her ascension stopped marching and watched as Borea rose higher as the chlorinated air grew disturbed all around her. As a collective, The People pointed at Borea as she continued to ascend.

The first thing to fall when the wind came was the flag. It was swallowed by the oblivion to the west. As the north wind grew into an omnipresent cyclone, blonde hair was torn from eugenically-approved scalps and spun like straw in a dust devil. Ivory skin was pulled from aesthetically pleasing bodies and The People were flayed alive all together. Their screams were melded into a single note in the wind not worth annotating. The crystal water of the river plummeted up into the abyss and shattered the dome as the heavier elements followed. When nothing was left but an earthen palette and the waterless channel, Borea finally blinked. Nothing but the bones from the macabre bridge remained and were buried with quick care by a few more gusts of the north wind. By the time Borea's feet touched the bare earth, the sun was shining but the clouds were gathering.

When she closed the ancient oak door behind her, Borea was soaked and the north wind was abating. It would be a century-long storm, the deluge of deluges no meagre book could record. As she ascended the stairs, her weariness proved that nobody would be awake to see it. Borea realized the only certainty was her bed and the window and dreams. The waking world had proven to be finite. Kronos had been banished long ago but his power lingered still. Entropy was the Titan who never fell. Borea felt like little more than an idle breath in a universe tending towards absolute zero. When she closed her eyes in bed, she stared out the window and watched the maelstrom obliterate space. As the twilight of waking and dreaming was upon her, Time fell dead just outside her window.

The Wall

by Eric Thralby

There is a wall made of muscle.
It is as if there were a shoulder pressing into a leg, wrapped
under a pair of arms, and a back bent in many segments. It is
twenty feet tall.
If one takes a flashlight under the crease of two long muscles
near the ground, one sees the shine of an eye.
We hear its muscles twisting up at night.
It is left to me to talk the wall out of existence.
Hello, Mr. Wall? We do not want you around anymore.
Is it the children? Tell them I'm only a wall.
It's actually everyone. You are too horrendous. The birds are
dropping dead from the sky. They are too afraid of the ground.
Our grandmothers are afraid to make jam. They look at their
own hands kneading the jam and they weep.
The wall twists like a man checking his heel.
I cannot move, I am a wall.
I've seen you swat a bird.

The Mother Dome

by Maev Barba

As my mother is equally afraid of small spaces as she is of large spaces, I will build my mother a geodesic dome, its outer wall comprised of two walls, essentially a dome over a dome, three feet of space between the two domes. The dome is then a very large space, but comprised of many small spaces. Because a geodesic dome is made up of many triangles and because—if the two domes are three feet apart—we may put narrow landings in every triangle, so that the inhabitant, or visitor, might sit, rest or hide in any one of the many triangles.

I am about six feet tall, but, bent in half, I fit in any triangle with three sides of three feet (area: 3.9 feet).

To make the geodesic dome, rows of slightly smaller triangles are arranged upon slightly larger triangles which are arranged below slightly smaller triangles, and on and on until the pattern forms a dome (this is oversimplified of course; in reality, the larger triangles form pentagons and the smaller triangles form hexagons and the dome is formed by rows of pentagons followed by rows of hexagons, and so on; but this does not change the fact that we're looking at triangles).

If my mother is able to reach up to feel with her hands something up to seven feet tall, then my mother will be able to reach up and feel around from any bottommost triangle to any second bottommost triangle. If I provide her with a stick, three feet in length, she will be able to poke around in any third level triangle.

Now, if it took my mother ten seconds to, in total darkness, determine whether or not I was inside any given triangle, and, if my mother went about this systematically (not wildly running triangle to triangle wherever her fear compels her, screaming and calling for me) checking triangle after triangle, it would take her thirty seconds to check each column, bottommost triangle to topmost triangle.

1. I will never hide in any triangle which my mother cannot reach.

2. I will never switch triangles at any point in the night. When darkness falls and I enter the dome, I pick one triangle and I stay in it.

3. On any given night, I may enter the dome from any direction and climb into any triangle, so long as I don't violate rules one or two.

My mother could then, within reason, examine two columns per minute, or, one-hundred and twenty columns an hour. If, given that this is the Pacific Northwest and at this time of year we have roughly eight hours every night of total darkness, I believe my mother could (again if she is rational and efficient) examine nine-hundred and sixty triangles per night.

On any given night then, my mother's odds of finding me are dependent totally on the size of the dome. Given a dome with the diameter of one hundred feet and the height of fifty feet, and therefore with the dome surface area of 15,707.96 feet, we divide 15,707.96 feet by the area of one triangle, so 15,707.96 feet divided by 3.9 feet, equalling 4027.68, rounding up to 4028 total triangles.

Given that my mother is only capable of searching the first three triangles in any given column, and given the diminishing number of triangles (a loss of six per hexagon every row moving up--the largest number at the bottom of the dome and the smallest number, being the dome's topmost point, one hexagon at the top), row-by-row, a dome with 4028 triangles, as my mother would only be capable of searching roughly ten percent (402 triangles) of the surface area of a dome fifty feet high (at 120 triangles examined per hour), it would take my mother less than half a night to examine every triangle in all three bottommost rows of the dome. Inevitably, she would find me.

Now, if we doubled the height and diameter of the dome (so, d=200 feet, h=100 feet) to get a dome surface area of 62,831.85, we then get 16,110.73 or, rounding up, 16,111 triangles. Searchability is diminished to seven percent because the dome is higher. My mother then is capable of searching 805 triangles. Again, piece of cake for my mother.

But if I design a dome one-thousand feet in diameter and five-hundred feet in height (dome surface area: 1,570,796.33 feet) then my mother must contend with 402,768 total triangles, five thousand searchable triangles, her chances of finding me in one night are reduced to roughly one night in five nights.

And a dome of one-hundred thousand feet in diameter and fifty-thousand feet in height (dome surface area:15,707,963,267.95 feet)? My mother has an estimated 5,034,604 searchable triangles.

A dome of 5,034,604 searchable triangles has a total volume of 261,799,387,799,149.4 cubic feet, the same volume as if Lake Michigan flooded Lake Huron.

In a dome of this size, my mother then, on any given night, has a 1 in 5594 chance in finding me. If she spends every night systematically examining triangles (maintaining her rate of 960 triangles examined per night), feeling around in every triangle in the dark, and poking at the upper triangles with a stick, I will see my mother only once every fifteen years.

Cutting the Mustard

by Hunter McLaren

I've been those half-bridges, those stone lions, those jittering
insect wings too. I've been that collapsing barn, *forgotten and
forgotten*
and forgotten. I've been the thing that rules everything,
or, I've been the things ruled, prices paid in full every time.

I've been that stepped-on cigar, gasping for oxygen and enough
fire,
I've been the lips that spat it too, breath stinking of eucalyptus
and whiskey.
I've been the impeding highways, pothole mouths gaping wide
for beaver fur and bird shit. Don't fear,

I've been windchimes, not the gentle kind, the untidy ones that
clang and
clang and clang until someone settles them, I've settled wind-
chimes too,
black out girls falling between toilets, glazed in their own lip
gloss
spit, I've been their green tequila drinks, two

straw shapes cut through me, my thinning blood. I've had a
mouse trap
for a tongue, gifted to me by a hunter, I only call to him when I
need
something, but he knows I've been something tricky, am still
something
tricky, am still smoothing out snow colored rabbit pelts.

The Homemade Spaceship
by Mickey Collins

We had some empty cardboard boxes from moving. We wanted to build something: a spaceship we decided. My brother got to choose, he wasn't older but he was in charge. I looked up to him. That's how we worked. He planned it all out, and I taped up the edges with packing tape where he said to. He stood above me and pointed with clean fingers. He was to be ground control and Buzz Aldrin and the rest of them all put together. My hands were splotchy red from tiny cardboard cuts and black from the permanent marker used to draw the buttons.

Through our hard work, it came together. We had a cockpit, which we didn't laugh at then, we were too young. You had to crawl through a box that once held a couch to get to the engine room. Another area served as the crew quarters, but we couldn't make bunk beds work so we just laid next to each other and talked as if he was above me. And our ship had four V-shaped wings. We even got to use the adult scissors, since NASA didn't use little kid scissors how could we.

It was cold in there too, which added to the believability. It was an unfinished room, concrete floors and when we closed the double doors it was dark. It was our personal outer space.

We visited Pluto, Uranus, the moon, Mars, Jupiter, and met with all sorts of aliens--action figures stood in for the real things. We could communicate with them when we had our translator, until our sister made us give her back her hairbrush. Then we would have to learn the language quickly or else cause an intergalactic war.

We were in that spaceship from the time after breakfast until lunch time. And then after lunch we played outside, while the spaceship stayed in the basement. Mom said we needed sunshine, we were too pale. Mom didn't even know that the sun was a star which was composed of hydrogen and helium and other gasses and the heat that we felt was radiation. All the while we thought of going back into that spaceship and my brother planned out our next adventure in chalk.

Every other weekend he spent with his dad. On those days the spaceship would sit idly by, floating in space. I didn't dare fly the ship without its captain.

And then one day, we had to retire our spaceship. The unfinished basement was to be finished and the "cardboard mess" was in the way, my dad said. My brother might have been the captain, but my dad was the admiral. Summer was ending soon anyways. We never did build another one, there was no place to put it.

My wife and I just moved into a new house. As I broke down a cardboard box to fit into the recycling bin, there it was. The two sides extended out like wings, and the front flap, that was the cockpit, and the flap in the back was the engines. I decided to call my brother. How long had it been?

Cats on Steam Pipe, Vilnius, Lithuania - Roger Camp 47

48 *Water Bolt - Mark Hurtubise*

Property Rights
by Phoebe Blanding

In my father's will, under **SURVIVORSHIP**, it reads, "any aforestated beneficiary of this will who dies within 30 days after my death shall be considered to have failed to survive me." My god, I think. Maybe he had a sense of humor after all. For a jarring, fleeting second, I entertain the possibility that within my father lurked some latent scrap of self-awareness. It's only legalese, yet it's apt. This is a test, a competition. Something I can fail. And I'm afraid I will. Driving the perilous curves of the 110, I see sparks and collisions, mangled metal like a premonition. Victory is tantalizingly close, but my grip is still tenuous. I clamp my hands tight on the wheel, worried that some part of me cannot be trusted.

His will leaves me everything there is to leave. "I'm an heir," I say, half-laughing, to my roommate, who calls me an *heiress* instead. I glower, but not for long. My roommate is refreshingly unfazed by my newfound half-orphan status. Absent heirs shall not inherit, I think, trying to remember the Latin. But I have, in my absence, inherited.

Thanks to something called a Ladybird deed, his house is mine the second they declare him dead. I am a property owner—an incongruous thought; I feel like it should be accompanied by a new accent. I wonder if the deed is named after the song, the one about the ladybug, with her burning house and imperiled children.

I've never been in the house. Haven't set foot in Michigan in years, not since well before he bought it. My roommate and I look it up a dozen or so hours after his death, open wine bottle on the table before us, clicking through photos from the last time it was for sale. Antlers on the wall, sunlight in the bedroom, snow in the yard. A little white clapboard house camouflaged against the snow. Quaint the way nothing in California could ever hope to be.

"Holy shit," I say, looking at the price, knowing I'll sell it and something close to that sum will be mine.

"Holy shit," my roommate says, because around here that

wouldn't buy you so much as the burnt-out carapace of a shack.

The house isn't the only thing that's mine to dispose of. His body is mine to do with what I will. They tell me he wanted it donated to science, but they need my consent. Now it matters if I say yes, if I say no. I could bulldoze over his wishes, stick him in a coffin, and plant him in the ground. I could burn him to ash and chuck him in the wretched concrete trickle of the L.A. River.

But I don't. I agree. The concept is faintly reassuring. I can't get it out of my head that capital-S Science is taking custody of him, and will determine what his fucking problem is. Was. I know, of course, that it doesn't work like that. Everything quantifiable has already been quantified. Plenty was wrong with his body. Knowing what it was never helped me any. Still, I can't shake the idea of Science, white-coated and objective, wielding scales and calipers, staring down the problem until it's tamed, reduced to nothing but the neat march of numbers.

On the puddle-jumper from O'Hare to Grand Rapids, I envision the wings of the plane snapping off; de-oxygenated, high-altitude air rushing in; the water of the Great Lake swallowing steel and flesh alike. But I'm calm. There's nothing I can do to stop it, yes, but there's also nothing I can do to make it happen.

Assuming the plane lands, I have four days ahead of me. I didn't go to the funeral because there wasn't one. I braced myself for hostile stares from strangers who share my DNA, ready for that familiar bubble of space and silence around me. I'm ashamed to admit it, but I feel like I've been denied my martyrdom. Instead, I'm out here to settle his affairs—namely, to sell his house, which is no longer his, but mine.

The plane doesn't crash. This doesn't seem like much of a reprieve when I emerge into the Gerald Ford International Airport. The "international" component strikes me as unlikely, but, on the other hand, presumably the natural reaction to finding oneself in Grand Rapids is to attempt to get as far away as possible. It's certainly how I want to respond. But what I want and what I do are two very different things. Instead of fleeing, I rent a car for the first time. I've been old enough to do so for thirteen days. My father's death was an early birthday present, though I honestly expected him to will himself into dying on my birthday, just to ensure it would always be about him. But he hadn't. Four days from now, I will have survived him, officially, like he is a hurricane, or typhus. Four days, I remind myself at the car rental kiosk, when the woman behind the counter glances at the collection of pins on my backpack, her gaze landing on the centerpiece, a button declaring that, "I gave my love to Jesus, but now He never calls." Only four, I repeat once I'm behind the wheel. Like when the window is up I'll be safe, no longer responsible for my own well-being. After I win, who gives a shit? I'm the victor.

Around me, the license plates read "Pure Michigan." Initially, I laugh, blink like I might be hallucinating. But I keep seeing it—car after car, even on a billboard, amplified. The message sinks in: I am not sufficiently pure. I am not prepared for what I'm getting myself into, waltzing east with Californian bravado, like these people are all too bland to hurt me. I should know better. My decision to come here was an ill-considered confluence of whim and obligation; only now does the reality sink in. I'm driving east from the airport when I should be fleeing the fuck back to the West Coast.

My concern over the figurative wrong direction I'm going in swamps my mind, and I'm slow to realize that I'm also going in the literal wrong direction. I tell myself I know this, like I'll snap a roadmap onto childhood memories of brief, tense visits, or head to my father's hometown by instinct, like a salmon.

No instincts are forthcoming. I start seeing signs for Muskegon and have to admit I've fucked up. After trying in vain to start directions on my phone one-handed, I pull into a grocery store parking lot. It's a Meijer, and the glow of the sign seems both an affront and an omen. I'm out of my element. The sight of a Wal-Mart would be welcome, Target virtually cosmopolitan. With shamefully tremulous fingers, I divest myself of pins and buttons. It had seemed so easy to be steadfast, to raise both middle fingers at them all, but I'd forgotten that I'd be alone. Alone, feeling like the entire state is scrutinizing me through narrowed eyes. I'd forgotten how little being right matters, sometimes. Maybe this is the wrong approach. Maybe defying them is only another way of giving them what they want—an excuse to shake their heads. I should've scrounged up some suitable spouse, a beige blob of respectability. The shock on

their faces might be worth it. Not that I have a suitable candi-
date on hand, but that's why Craigslist was invented. Though
to really sell it, I'd need a baby, and those must be considerably
harder to procure, though I've always had an intrepid streak,
so—

I cut myself short. You hate these people, I remind myself.
You hate them back, glare for glare, sneer for sneer. You don't
want to be what they want you to be.

Still, I leave the pins scattered on the seat and follow
the GPS to the house, which is grayish in the fading light, the
lawn around it reduced to dead patches and bare dirt. I get the
key from the obviously fake rock sitting conspicuously on the
otherwise-empty doorstep. As soon as I open the door and flip
on the light, I know I've made a mistake. I'd expected the house
from the real estate photos, not this husk. It isn't empty like an
ad, a blank slate. That would be better. There's some furniture
crowded together in the middle of the room. It gives me the
impression that the objects have huddled together for warmth.
But that isn't what convinces me that I've fucked the fuck up by
coming here. It's me. Or, rather, it's my face. I'm already here,
snapped and shot and framed and nailed to the walls, too many
versions of my face smiling the same tense, unwilling nod in the
direction of a smile—the pained crook of my lips as they fight a
snarl, a sneer. Trapped deer eyes, dark glint of anger deadened
by the paper's gloss. I'm already here, haunting this house. My
father has been keeping me here. I count nine photos, nine me's,
staggered at various ages, clone-like Von Trapps gathered to
watch him.

He's dead. I'm alive. I'm the only part of him that's still
living. Suddenly, this feels like his victory. My cells are half his,
encoded with what he was. My mouth turns sour, and I swallow
saliva that feels more his than mine.

Cramming the key in my pocket, I barrel out the door,
fumbling to get the car unlocked and started. I pull out in a
careless squeal of tires, making turns that would be dangerous if
there was anybody around for me to crash into. But there isn't,
and I make it to the grocery store unscathed. Another Meijer,
smaller than the first. I can't remember if they sell alcohol in
grocery stores here, but I walk purposefully, afraid to give off a
lost aura—permission to approach, offer help that isn't the sort

I need. I assess my options. I want something that burns, but I'll take what I can get, so I grab a bottle of wine by the neck. The label is vaguely Goth, which is good enough for me. My skin crawls as the cashier studies my I.D. Seeing, I'm suddenly sure, wrongness. Otherness. An outsider with a familiar surname.

Telling myself I should preserve my sanity by getting a hotel room, I drive back to the house. I tear through the living room, bypassing the crowd of my staring faces. The kitchen, at least, is unlikely to have my likeness plastered all over it. But I don't know the floorplan and loop—dangerously, it seems—towards the bedroom before reorienting myself and landing in the kitchen. No copies of me here. No utensils, either. The cupboards are empty, standing open. I close the nearest one by instinct, a pinched, uninvited voice from childhood echoing through my head. *If you leave the cupboards open, people will talk about you.* I'd never known if this was a superstition, like throwing salt over your shoulder or not giving knives as gifts, or meant literally—neighbors whispering behind cupped palms about your slovenly ways. Asking felt too risky, so I didn't. It doesn't matter, anyway. In this town, they're talking about me behind my back, no matter the state of the cupboards.

His sisters have gone through the house. I was informed; it isn't supposed to be a violation and I'm not supposed to be surprised. I just hadn't anticipated that they'd empty all the drawers, all the cupboards. That they would take the forks, whisking them off to wherever the forks of the dead go.

Maybe he never had forks. I could believe he lived like that. What I can't buy, however, is that he didn't own a corkscrew. I glance at the bottle in my hand, fleetingly optimistic, but it confirms what I already knew: not a screwtop. I check the empty drawers, the vacant cupboards with liners peeling at the edges, blue flowers under dust. Empty, empty, empty. They've been thorough. I'm thorough, too. I can feel the absence, the bottles I know they've taken away. One of the few images I can conjure of the time I spent around my father. Empties, the recycling piled high, white-yellow labels on clear plastic.

Taking a deep breath, I try to strategize. My overstuffed backpack sits by my feet, and I grab it, thinking I might be able to extract the cork with a pocketknife. My hands are already rooting in the bag when I remember: the fucking TSA. All my weapons laid out on the bed before I left. I've been disarmed.

"I'll go back to the store," I say to the ransacked kitchen, but my breathing is unsteady. My skin burns preemptively at the thought of walking under those fluorescent lights, weapon-less, where they can see me, where in any crowd of more than a dozen there's probably a second cousin of mine lurking.

My hands keep digging in the backpack. Reflex, instinct, something. They come up, not empty, but holding a jumbo sharpie. I eye the marker, the bottle. My hands, like this is a plot they've hatched.

Sinking to the floor, I peel the foil from the bottle's neck with my fingernails. I have the inexplicable sensation that I'm buying myself time. Removing the foil soothes me, but not enough. Lining the end of the sharpie up with the top of the cork, I press tentatively. Nothing. I draw back, then try again, putting some weight into it. Just when I'm ready to withdraw, I feel it start to give. Invigorated and hopeful, I lean harder, but the bottle skids sideways, tipping over. I catch it, one-handed, before it hits the floor. My travel-sullied hair clings to the back of my neck; it feels greasier than it did when I started. I resettle the sharpie atop the cork, which may have sunk a centimeter or two. Pinning the wine bottle between my legs, I shove the sharpie against the cork with all the force I can muster.

It moves slightly, and I have just enough time to think "holy shit" before the cork plunges into the bottle and I lose my balance, slipping forward as wine sprays up at me. I sit back, blinking wine off my eyelashes as it trickles down my cheeks and forehead. My legs and the linoleum are equally splattered. These are the only jeans I brought, so I guess I'll be spending the rest of my time in Michigan smelling like halfway-decent grocery store wine. Lifting the bottle, I drink, only slightly impeded by the cork, which is trapped inside and bobbing unhelpfully. My front teeth clank against the glass. Wine sloshes out, missing my mouth and landing on my neck. I imagine the sight I make, what they'd all think if they could see me. Slowly, a grin overtakes my face, until I'm beaming into the dark of the hallway, like everyone really is there to watch. Like he's watch-ing, too. Here, I think, taking another swig. Take my fucking picture now.

Twelve Things
by L. Fid

Twelve is a magic number.

Two is knowledge, duality,
  a cleaving and clarity.

Eight is a hope against.

Nine is the repentstation.

Five is the stake.

Four is the building

Six is a surprise.

Seven is change.

Ten is then.

Eleven goes nowhere, isolated,
  alone, forgotten dead.

Three is the magic number.

One is all.

Thirteen screams: SCREW ALL THAT!!!

Is it over, is it done,
  when it stops
and does not start?

Will they know us,
  when we've come,
if the names don't match,
  and the numbers subtract?

Living Structures

by Nicholas Yandell

1. Down Below:

Silver tube speeding,
Blurs of blues and whites,
Bricks and dark.

Open cavernous lairs,
For seasoned daily travelers,
Absorbed in ignoring liminal surroundings,
Minds already docked to destinations,
Hooking in place that final link.

With a scream to a stop,
And a chime to begin,
Towing them away,
Through final moments,
Of humming headphones,
And worn-out Sudoku books,
Or staring into smeared mirrors,
From drugstore makeup containers,
Recalling daytime ravages,
Before eyes drifting up,
To carefully chosen words on the wall.

Gently idling,
Thoughts steady,
Until a surfacing moment,
The jolt of a stop,
Where we can silence,
The waking motor,
And garble the voice,
Of the great pretender,
Pulling breath into consciousness.

Pausing.

To acknowledge freely,
That we actually are autonomous,

From the great moving machinery,
That barrels through,
These deepest recesses of night.

2. Ground Level:

I could disappear,
As just a streak,
In rivers of clothes and skin,
But how long have I been walking?

These straight roads,
Are the only ways I've ever known.

Growing up,
With dusty trails as mentors,
Guiding me past the horizon,
With an itch to escape,
The binds of familiarity,
And unwind the long tether of home.

Now thrown,
With the vaguest sense of exposure,
Traversing the wilderness,
Of a concrete labyrinth,
Leaving trepidation stalled,
In shadow alley,
To find the motion,
In the moonlight,
Of empty parking lots.

Thrust onward,
On the cement tracks,
With the long vertical lines,
And pulsing commands,
Floating above,
My broken mirrored movements,
Shattering the squares,
Of programmed civilization,
Where the through is clear,
But the purpose is cloudy.

Disperse.

The rising steam,
To another world,
Beckons me,
Beyond light's riddled paths,
And the waning flare,
Of my odyssey,
In the surface realm.

3. Up Above:

Lost in the city,
Except for my imagination,
As an able architect,
Scaling monoliths,
Interacting with imprisoned daylight,
Between the shadows of giants,
Grappling with gravity,
Opening eyes that haunt,
The stone flesh and steel bones.

Sculpting air,
Into restless columns,
Propping up the clouds,
Coaxing the breath of civilization,
Into rhythms of the music,
Filling the atmosphere.

Dividing the evening sky,
Folding up the sheets,
Of this star-studded canvas,
Before slipping them,
Discreetly,
Into my pocket.

Envisioning this scene,
That existed once,
As just a spark of ambition,
Incited,

By wandering the roads,
With eyes to the stratosphere,
And a deep dream,
Embedded within.

Envelope
by Peter Waldor

You find a long dried
bouquet of wild daisies
and asters, yellow daisies,
purple asters, the daisy
petals folded back
like a comet's tail.
The aster petals are gone
and you pinch
the globe of seeds
and drop them into
an envelope never to
hold a check or love letter,
separating the seeds
between thumb and pointer
with the same gentle action
as pinching salt on a delicacy.
There is a barren hillside
and though it's late
in autumn you say it's not
too late, or at least they can
rest there until spring.

Springtime
by Holly Day

the river cracks awake in the middle of the night, sounds like something
falling inside the house, sounds like the dog/kid broke some-
thing. I get up
so he doesn't have to, stomp out into the living room bathed in
bright moonlight, see
the dog curled up by the front door, oblivious to whatever woke
us up.

From the living room, I can hear more ice breaking off, feel the
river waking up
Pushing trapped branches and dead deer off to the side banks,
determined
To become an unhindered body once more. From the bedroom,
my husband asks
What's going on. I don't know where to start.

The Architecture of the Apple Tree

by Timothy Arliss O'Brien

As she was chasing the apple down the hill she wondered if the day could get any better. Her sojourn through the desert depleted her of the most important things. Those people who deplete every thought of identity one could find important.

The sky looked down on her like a mother bear, protective and soft; angry and violent. Times like this when she was alone reminded her of the possibilities to be anyone. Anywhere.

That one time we found that money on the ground and spent it on happiness.
Hopefully I won't remember that night.

Some people come here just to hate us. Some people don't understand themselves and get offended at the way life happens. "We all have choices, but yours are not as important as theirs. And don't ever you forget that darling."
The most fucked up thing I've heard.

She only loved him as much as she could.
Her brain didn't handle it.
Cosmic.
Catalyst.
Catatonic.

Is he happy now? Oh yes he is.
You have no idea how he blossomed. The sky was a better protector for him than it will ever be for you.
Sadness knows no bounds as it did for her.

But now he is
L
O
V
E
D.

We can move on.
We can hold hands.
We may be happy.
(We have permission.)

The things that are important talk to us louder,
and speak to us kinder,
and show us our value better.

Believe you me,

We will be fine and we have already eaten the apple.

No one can ever poison us.

64 *Stormtrooper's Apprentice - Mark Hurtubise*

Reflections on Tower Living

by Azalea Micketti

5.

I remember the cold stones against my toes. I remember the roughness of the wooden door frame beneath my fingers. I remember the jagged indentation in the floor, the one that perfectly fit the pad of my thumb, that became smooth and soft with years of worrying. I remember pressing my ear to the wall hard enough that the shell of my ear suctioned to the stone, and wondering if I would be able to hear if anyone came close. Or if the stones themselves would warn me if I listened hard enough.

I did hear things while I sat there in the dark. Voices that were not my own, whether from memory or madness I was never sure. These voices whispered things, shared their dreams, told me stories. I was raised as much by their words as I was by the cold stone around me. The darkness eventually began to show me things as well. The shadows took shape, pictures forming and reforming, history repeating itself over and over. This is how I learned to speak, to sing. This is how I learned to listen and observe. This is how I learned to mimic and remember.

And the stones did warn me. I heard them coming, and heeded the warning to cover my eyes before the door was even opened. Sometimes I wonder what they thought when they first saw me, those mysterious door openers. I never saw them; they were gone by the time I could open my eyes. The first person I saw was one I recognized from the shadow stories.

Those memories are all dark and distant, because the room was in a near constant state of darkness and because I was young. Too young, I now know. Or maybe not young enough.

4.

My second seemed like a luxury compared to my early days.

First, there were windows. Two of them.

The windows were too high to see out of, but the light and

the air and the feeling of being human was novelty enough. It wore off eventually, but I never forgot the swell inside my chest when I first stepped into that room.

The sunshine reflecting on the warm wood floor was the most beautiful thing I had ever seen. There were a hundred thousand colors layered into the grain of the wood, and depending on the time of day the sun would paint them with even more. Everything sparkled and there was more variation and nuance than I had ever imagined in my life.

I used to lie in that beam of light and doze like a cat. And when I wasn't dozing I would count the grain lines in the floor, or watch the dust dance through the sunbeam. And for the first time I noticed change in my surroundings. The sun would rise and set, the shadows it made moving slowly across the wall, moving in a slow dance with the shadows who had stayed with me. The temperature would fluctuate with what I now know were seasons. All I knew then was the fact of the cool floor against my cheek and the blanket (that had been a new word to learn) over my chest. I saw the places the sun touched the wall change from day to day. I learned that other people slept when it was dark and rose when the sun did. I had never had anything to measure my time before and it was an odd sensation.

I learned to read in that room. Through the combined efforts of the voices and a nurse I learned swiftly, and devoured book after book. I learned that my darkness was not the same as other people's. I learned to see myself in the way other people looked at me. I slept in my first bed. That was one I was sad to leave, because for the first time it felt like mine, like I had changed a place by being in it.

The feelings there are still mostly fond ones.

3.

For the first time I was not alone.

I was never truly alone, for I always had my voices and the shadows. But never had I been forced to engage with others on a daily basis. Surrounded by young ones my own age, it was impossible to sleep. I had lived my life to that point listening to very little except the sound of whispered voices, my own breath and heartbeat. And suddenly I heard every single heartbeat in that room, pounding nearly as loudly as my own. Every single shift and shuffle: skin against fabric, wood against stone, the crunch of straw, the gasping lungs and the grumbling stomachs, the midnight tears and the whispered conversation.

I learned about language. Some people used different words, entirely different sounds, to describe the same thing. There were some things, some experiences, we had no words for at all. And yet others we had words for but were not supposed to say. That sometimes people could not understand each other, even when they spoke the same language. I learned that not everyone heard the voices from the stone and wood and air.

I learned that words had an unknown power to shape the lives around me. Some of the young ones took words very seriously, while others threw them away. I collected as many words as I was able, learning how to string them together in a myriad of different languages and patterns. Words that caused pain, words that healed wounds, words that brought tears and joy in equal measure. Words that lay the dead to rest, and words that brought back memories repressed over many lifetimes.

Pain taught me that not all words need to be repeated.

Never in my life had I felt more isolated than when I was surrounded by other people.

I could see the others look at me differently than they did each other. Especially after I took the straw filled mattress off of my tiny cot and slid it underneath the wooden bed frame.

I slept better after that. I felt safer with something over my head. Less exposed. And it helped to soften the noise. A little.

2.

The fourth one was not my choice.

None of them had been, but it's different when you don't know you have a choice.

The polished wooden floor, the silk sheets on a bed three times the size of any I had seen, the personal fireplace, the four (yes four) floor to ceiling windows, the mahogany wardrobe ready to fill with belongings I did not have, the ten foot silver mirror that reflected anything but my own image.

I had never felt more trapped.

This luxury was misplaced and ill-used. I could see out of these windows, of course I could. I could see the life I would be missing. I could see the people I could not touch. I could see the countryside I would never visit. And my voices could describe it to me in exquisite detail. It was the best and worst place I had ever been.

This is where I learned to weave everything I had learned together, literally and figuratively.

I learned to weave the tapestries that were so prized by so many, none of them knowing exactly where they came from. I wove the stories in gold and silver thread, in deep eggplant and striking scarlet. I embellished them with embroidery till my fingers bled, and then I wove some more. I learned to spin my own thread from wool and darkness, and I learned how to touch each fiber with memory until it sparkled. I learned how to create the most beautiful stories in the world, and I learned that I would never be in them.

To have a taste of a life I have never known, without the option to choose it. It was not on my terms, it would never be on my terms. I could have all these things, the only thing I could not have was myself.

From this place I saw eternity pass me by. I wove it into pictures. I learned of the hubris, the caprice, the cruelty, and the unbelievable arrogance of the world. But I also learned of its desire, its compassion, its selfless joy, and its love.

It was unbearable.

To see the world and be unable to participate. To record the mistakes of others without being able to help. To hear of the adventure and the great deeds without the option to add my own to the list. I never saw myself. I saw my handiwork every-where, but never the person who had created it.

Until I saw you.

Looking at me from my mirror, out of my tapestry, up at my window.

There you were. Over and over and over.

And I knew it was time for this to end.

1.

When I threw myself from that tower, I never dreamed there would be another one.

I fell from a great height, understanding and expecting it to be the last I would see and feel of this world.

Instead I woke floating down the river I myself had described countless times in blue and gray and purple threads.

I woke to a broken neck, unable to feel my toes. I breathed out and sank, feeling only relief as the water closed over my head.

I woke to a face, blurry and far away. Calling out to me. I fell under again.

I woke to a bed. To one of my own pieces hanging on the wall.

I woke to sunset and music, and a figure in the corner of the room.

0.

I awoke to you.

The only person who has looked and seen me, not merely what they want from me.

I woke to another tower. This one not so high, nor so fine, but much closer to the home I used to have. Warm, quiet, full of light. Not a prison or a cage, but a choice.

You gave me everything, and asked nothing in return. You showed me compassion, helped me learn to move again on my own, and then gave me the choice: to stay, to go, to come back.

That is what I choose: to make my own way, to participate, to find, to learn, to be. To come back.

Always to come back.

Medford Looming

by AJD

Leaving Ashland, mountain fairies
Packed my lunch
Vegan fare
Medford looming, Medford dooming
Mill town, pill town
Overpass
Exit thirty to sixty-two
Lava Lanes, cow dance road house
No city, meth city, White City
Assembly line, swing shift, unincorporate
Wage slave trailer tears
No escape
Medford looming, Medford dooming

Glass Spectacle

by John Chrostek

Overnight, a studio apartment made entirely of glass appeared in the middle of the waterfront park. Every surface, every wall, every piece of furniture within (save a single pillar of stone in the dead center of the room) was made of the same sturdy, translucent glass. From the outside there was no nook or cranny hidden from the public eye, no respite from curiosity. There was also no door out, no hatch or window to the outside world. Air circulated in from small holes by the ceiling so that, if unable to escape, the famous artist Raulo Pagratis would at the very least not suffocate to death on public land.

Word spread quickly. By midday, the apartment had attracted a small crowd of onlookers.

"What's this all about?"

"Hey! You in the box!"

But Raulo, if he heard them, did not answer. He avoided eye contact with the onlookers, committing to carving down the stone pillar or sitting in his chair of polished glass to rest. Curious onlookers would wait and watch, hoping to uncover clues to his intention here, but he revealed nothing, signalled nothing. He continued his pattern of action until the sun hung low in the sky, and most of the crowd had dissolved. That was when he first used the shower.

Within an hour, local law enforcement had arrived at the scene. Long since toweled off, Raulo had transitioned to reading a tome of a book kept beside his bed of glass. The police circled off the perimeter, shining auto-spotlights and tapping the glass to get the artist's attention (to request to see his permits, to ask to contain displays of public nudity) but all he offered were brief and furious glances before returning to his insular world. This, of course, did nothing to de-escalate tension with the police, and soon the situation had become a primetime media circus replete with helicopter footage blaring across local media networks.

At 8:18 pm, a small man in a three-piece suit arrived on

the scene carrying a manila folder and a small sign. Before his presence was noted, he had hammered the sign down into the grass just in front of the structure. The sign read:

Raulo Pagratis (b. 1967)

Raulo Pagratis, 2020

Flesh & Stone in Glass

Waterfront Park Exhibition Space (*Glasshaus*)

The man was Artur Palotz. To an audience of armed police, Artur demonstrated the preparedness and decorum that had led him twenty years prior to be named Raulo's most esteemed assistant. In quick order, he procured from his folder the necessary documentation that proved that Raulo's current exhibition had been legally permitted, taking care to underline and note the specific legalese that protected him against retaliation in the issues of public nudity, zoning laws, and fire code standards. The officer in charge, Sergeant Deborah Glade, marvelled at the documents, listening intently to Artur's methodic breakdown of his client's situation in regards to landmark legal cases of the past fifty years. It was as if Artur had traveled ahead to the future, sat through lengthy court proceedings compiling notes, only to return to his original timeline and systematically eliminate all proven room for error. Deborah knew that, if a case could still be made, it could not be won through the heavy hand of intimidation, and dispersed her frustrated entourage into the waiting evening.

"I would ask you to remind your client that there is a middle way between performance art and expensive, uncooperative demonstrations. It would never have escalated like this if we had been informed ahead of time," she offered in parting.

"Everything is to his liking," Artur replied. "One can never do everything correctly."

Artur and Raulo did not speak before Artur took his leave. Raulo spent his first night in the Glasshaus beneath a clear and starry sky, alone save a lone vagrant who set up camp in the periphery.

By the next morning, the Glasshaus had become a destination. The previous day's debacle had been disseminated among the city's well-to-do, and the museum scene was ecstatic at the surprise launch of an installation by one of the art world's biggest names. The confrontation with the police also attracted local anarchists and crust punks, who believed that Raulo's action was either a revolutionary resistance of state authority or a dedicated satire of cultural institutions that had attempted to confine art and remove it from public space. Needless to say, tensions between the two camps ran high. The elite staked out the river-facing side of Glasshaus for themselves with crimson stanchions, leaving the inland side to the astoundingly quick growing tent city. From within his studio, Raulo paid no mind to it all, or pretended so, single-mindedly continuing the slow labor of his project.

"The artist is trying in his way to convey the claustrophobia of today's ever-present media culture and its effect on the individual soul. His sculpture within the space represents the sanctity of true expression on a ravenous world stage that seeks to affect the end result every step of the way!" The voices ruminated.

"By surrendering all privacy in a voyeuristic human zoo of his own making, Raulo is showing us how simple and animalistic the act of creation is!"

"Who is bringing him food? Has anyone seen someone bring him food?"

"He's gonna use the toilet again, it's getting late, let's go."

For several days, the space around the display took on a festival atmosphere. On the river walkway, booths were set up advertising municipal events and selling hastily-printed t-shirts. A Peruvian food cart was the first to get a permit for the area, quickly becoming an unofficial part of the experience. The owner, Marcielo Quispe, took the city by storm with her citrus zest ceviche, which hundreds of happy patrons agreed paired wonderfully with the experience of sitting in a field and watching a famous old man carve at stone from a giant glass box.

Multiple local and national news outlets, over the peak days of the exhibit, tried to get an interview with Raulo. When that failed, they scoured the city, the globe, for anyone who could provide soundbites that illuminated the artist's intentions.

Somehow, the esteemed Artur Palotz was able to stay completely out of view, and no immediate family members or friends revealed themselves. The mystique prevailed, but mystique without payoff is a drug the masses quickly build a tolerance to. The decay of novelty, coupled with a few days of intermittent rain spelled the end of the exhibit's golden period in the public eye.

The statue within the Glasshaus was nowhere near done.

Days passed, one as much like the other. The Peruvian food cart, Chilly Hen, still attracted waterfront park goers, who would chuckle as they leaned against the river railing, watching the artist move about in his open, private world. The anarchist punks hung about for some time, resisting the city's efforts to displace them. The space became an Occupy-style art space, pungent with the smell of unwashed bodies, where long-haired crust punks and vagrants played banjo and sold paintings and jewelry. Tensions regarding the divide were of concern to the police, who were still under municipal pressure not to affect the newsworthy exhibition with flashy displays of violence.

It was around supper time on a Friday two weeks into the exhibition when a woman and daughter came to the waterfront park. Chewing lamb kebabs, they walked up to the open grass around the Glasshaus and sat down. Raulo had spent most of the day reading one of the books he had somehow brought with him into the studio, barely touching the pillar that had now roughly begun to resemble the shape of a human body.

The pair watched Raulo for twenty minutes in silence read his large book until his eyes rose to meet them. He twitched in his chair, his book falling to the ground. The daughter looked to the mother, who gave her a comforting nod. Raulo rose from his chair as if despite himself, on automatic. He walked up to the edge of the glass, the two women meeting his gaze.

"Why is he looking at us like that?" The daughter asked, uncomfortable.

"Because it's very lonely in that box," the mother offered.

"Why doesn't he just get out?"

"He built it for himself. There aren't any doors."

"I don't understand."

"Of course you don't, my little songbird. You're clever and you're free."

Raulo watched them finish their kebabs. The daughter ran off towards the river, and he watched her go with gentle pain. The mother stayed behind for just a moment in the gravity of Raulo. Their eyes met. Raulo's hand pressed against the glass. He feigned a kind of smile, an intimate, obvious lie. The woman shook her head, her posture calm but firm. Raulo pointed to his chest and raised his gaze outwards, towards the distant child. Again, the woman shook her head. He sighed and nodded, his fingers sliding down the cold interior glass.

By this point, the few stragglers around the Glasshaus had noticed something strange was transpiring, and had begun to congregate about the structure. The woman gave a fleeting second more to Raulo, who had retreated further into the habitat. He was now looking all about him, as if waking from a vigorous sleepwalk. When he looked back, the woman in the grass had vanished, the dedicated observers throwing pebbles at the studio to catch his eye. Raulo sat back down in his glass chair, his red leather tome still sprawled on the floor of his workspace. He did not move again for hours.

Weeks passed. Over time, the block of stone was whittled down, bit by bit, into what was obviously a statue of Raulo himself. The figure of Raulo was nude, holding up a bitten apple in the sunlight. If the public had not become slowly desensitized to the image of Raulo naked, the precise, unflattering details might have created some discomfort. Instead, to those who checked in to watch the artist work, the Glasshaus had become a modest, if overwrought testament to the artist's skill and showmanship, with the vulnerability and transparency edging out most criticisms of his obvious exhibitionist flair.

"I've never seen a man work so hard to normalize the image of his penis," a college student joked, passing by the Glasshaus with an entourage of stoned cohorts.

"He really hasn't left that box in months? Has he seen a doctor?"

"You know he's sneaking out at night when no one's looking. He has to be."

Raulo looked up from his work on the contours of the left shin. He bared his teeth like an ape, the fleshy sockets of his eyes deep and wild canyons.

That night, almost none of the normal squatters remained. The twin camps of the Glasshaus had fallen quiet. The stanchioned riverside was lit by gentle string lights, barren and underutilized in preparation for the final completion of the exhibition, when it would at last again be of newsworthy significance. On the inland side, the police had long since run out the anarchist commune, leaving behind the blasted and broken wreckage of tents, beds, kilns, and baths. Hand-made pamphlets decrying the violence of the state and Raulo's silent acceptance fluttered like butterfly corpses in the cold breeze coming in from the river. From the darkness, the long-forgotten Artur congealed into being. Raulo met him by the glass wall facing the park's interior.

"You are holding up well, I hope," Artur began.

Raulo nodded.

"Are you prepared?"

Again.

"I will have the ship waiting at the community dock a quarter mile to the west. We have prepared passage for you into international waters. The world will believe you have vanished. You have no desire to change that plan, yes?"

Raulo nodded, a smile on his lips. He had stayed strong for this, the promise of perfect escape.

"Very well. Be sure to secure the trap door tightly on your departure. Otherwise, the tank will leak and the piping we installed will have been worthless."

Raulo laughed. He put his hand on the glass. Artur raised his hand to meet him.

"It has been an honor serving your art, old friend."

Raulo's eyes shone with gratitude.

"Very well. I must be off. Prepare yourself," Artur commanded, before vanishing again into the waiting night.

Two hours later, the lone vagrant, Raulo's most enduring companion in the waterfront park, stumbled back into the area. He had just traded an iPhone for a baggie of smack and was in a sunken world of his own making, enjoying a stilted walk beneath the stars. Night after night, he was drawn to the glow of the Glasshaus. He enjoyed watching Raulo, feeling as if the artist was a person of the world in a manner like himself. There were always eyes on him, too, a thousand eyes and one, he could feel them in the shadows and the buildings.

When he arrived at the Glasshaus, something had changed. Water had somehow gotten in. The vagrant, with the uneven gait of a man halfway to heaven, stepped closer. All the man's belongings were floating in the water. Loose papers, books, glass furniture circling in the slow whirl as the Haus had filled up to the air holes and run over. At the center of it all stood the statue of Raulo, still holding his bit apple on high, unburdened by the crushing pressure of the water. It was only after stepping closer that Raulo himself could be seen, his hands gripped tightly on a latch on the floor of the Glasshaus. He was not moving. His eyes and mouth were open.

The vagrant knocked on the glass, but Raulo did not answer. He knocked again. No response. This was all quite tiring. He walked over where the grass was dry and sat down. From the river nearby came the sound of a trawler's motor coming to life, idling for a long moment, then at last driving off westward towards the awaiting sea. The vagrant did not turn to watch it go. He stared straight ahead, mesmerized by the statue of Raulo glimmering and breathing in the moonlight and LEDs. He had never seen anything so real.

Hymn for the Coffin
by Hunter McLaren

I shatter with that night hiding inside my horns, when

        you tried to teach me the mausoleum dance, how to
behold myself on glassy marble graves, but I wasn't

        listening. I draped rugs across my back and lied
about being heavy. I bite with that morning hiding in

      my gums, when I asked you to make me pearls, forgetting
they were yours to begin with, yours for the taking, not

        my deafening treasures to clutch tightly.
I live with when the word FAG cliff dove from my throat

      down into my gut, leaving a trail of lit matches on the
way, when I thought about taking garden shears across

      the metal of your car, when I told people I was the axe.
I was really the lumberman. I said that being faultful wasn't

      my own, that it was God or an animal who made me
do things I lied about, tied in sacks, poured cement over,

        buried under the rotting treehouse.
I will die boxed up with these war-things too, it is my only fate.

The Anatomy of a Partition
by Jacob Davis

I don't know how
to speak of structure
when structure is a wall
wished into existence
some matter of will
prevailing against another
you went mad
you said
over a horse
being beaten
of all things
but I get it I
know the difference
between the
living
and the
dead.
Are you afraid of your Nation?
how can you be blamed
but I think you found
your own way
considering
the converse
of "keep out!"
is "stay in."

The Well
by Eric Thralby

There is a well with the voice of an older man. No one is sure
how long he's been in there.
I'm stuck down here, he says.
A pair of boys find him in the woods. They are the first in a
dozen years.
Does he crawl out at night? Does he crawl around like an eel?
They have a rope. They lower down into the well.
They feel their way around.
The walls are made of stones.
The man stirs and at first they cannot find him.

They see him in the low light.
I'm not well dressed, he says.
He looks ashamed.
That's ok, say the boys.
May we take a look around?
Be my guests, he says.
The older man leads them into a sub-tunnel within the pit.
They are maybe sixty feet below ground.

Along here is where I live, he says.
He shows them the few things that he has.
Some things have a crank. Some have a retractable part.
It's not lonely, he says.
He allows them into two opposite tunnels, each boy a tunnel.
Are you here? they say.
Yes, I'm here, he says.

Inside the tunnels, they could see their mothers.
Each boy watched his own mother drinking.
Eventually, they crawled into bed with their mothers.
And eventually they crawled back out from their tunnels.
Are you going to visit me again?
The older man's hands were wet, but not unlike a mother's.

The Fathers
by Bob Selcrosse

There is a culture where, when the men know it's time to die, climb trees.
They hope, upon death, to drop from the tree and explode on the ground.
The higher they fall the further spreads their progeny.

The job in boyhood is to identify your father.
Sons of honorable fathers must identify their fathers by their teeth.

There are the unfortunate few, however. Their father survives.
The father lands a cripple, a man broken on the ground.
And the son must drag his father. Home again, eventually they die shamefully as failures.

The hardiest of fathers do not take failure for an answer. They, broken legged, even broken armed, crawl back and climb and jump. They will crawl and climb and jump, as many times as it will take. These fathers are truly admired.

It is not for the son to drag his father. Save him the shame.
Beat your father. Scream at your father.
Do what it takes to get him back up that tree.

Dishonest children plead with their fathers at the bottoms of trees.
Deformed children, beg their fathers to climb.
Beggars, claim shamefully their fathers are somewhere still alive.

Suicide is not permitted. This is the death of a son before a father. This is the eradication of the family line.
No son may kill himself while his father is breathing.
Fathers will chase their sons through the woods with spears.
A father may wound the son and incapacitate him. Then, as if it were a race, he may outpace his son, scale the tree, and jump.

Distrustful children camp with a view of the tree in which their

father is hiding.
Some fathers bring supplies.
Sons keep an eye through binoculars and hurl feminizing curses
at their fathers.
These wily fathers are caught plucking nuts, eating birds, and
sticking their tongues out in the rain.

The sons of heroes walk their fathers.
They discourse upon mothers on their way to a tree.

There is a son who made a cloak to give his father on this day.
He wove it every night. A proper shroud of every color.
But then asked his father, Don't go.
No! Of course he must. It was his time.
He made his father eat a special dinner.
And let his father drink his favorite wine.
The father wore the cloak and climbed the tree.
His son held his foot and helped him reach a higher branch.

Upon three days, his father withered.
The highest tree in all the woods.
Upon the ground, he was unrecognizable.
Blessed by the gods.
The son built a grave above his father.
Around the grave he built a hut.
Upon the hut he thatched a roof.
Below the roof he heard the fathers.

They broke around him day and night.
They broke onto his roof or fell around it.
They broke from trees out in the distance.
They broke through many branches.

They climb the trees and die in leaves!
No son should build a hut.
Except for this brave father.
For he had jumped higher than anyone.

The Heptagon

by Hayden Moore

*'The beauty of a star-shaped figure—a hexagonal star, say—is
impaired if we regard it as symmetrical relatively to a given axis'
(Ludwig Wittgenstein)*

'I'm at sixes and sevens here…' Those were the last words
she remembered her grandfather saying before his end. The
words that followed were garbled consonants articulated by the
vowels of bile and halted breaths. Ever since that night almost
three years ago—a night crowned by madness and fear—Are-
thusa had latched onto those final words as a mendicant would
the handful of words heard from the divine in the midst of
desperate prayer. There was a tremendous gulf between six and
seven: Even and odd, unlucky and lucky, aligned and prime,
pure and cockeyed. Hexagons were the pinnacle of the geom-
etry of nature, the configuration par excellence, the always
duplicated but never repeated Platonic snowflake. Somehow,
her grandfather had latched onto a pair of numbers that had
nothing in common but proximity. All the rest was difference.
The girl felt her grandfather had presented her with some kind
of riddle, a riddle to help her carry on or one to drive her mad.
If the riddle was destined to drive her to madness, Arethusa
vowed to use her wits while they remained to find some bits of
the answer along the way.

The way was broken earth riddled with ice. If the earth
was speaking, its words were a random series of hard conso-
nants and nothing more. Fire was far more precious than food
or water. Fire made the ice submit and give up its liquid secret.
Fire attracted the creatures otherwise hidden in the depths
of the forest. Fire stirred something in the frozen instincts of
beasts and made them submit to their own sacrifice. The flames
that warmed Arethusa's fingers and face were the direct prog-
eny of the first fire set under the mouth of the cave. Its embers
had never faded. It was here that her grandfather had prayed to
Prometheus to give back the gift. A little spark from a pair of
stones restarted it all. As far as Arethusa knew, this was the only
fire left in the world. Seven years tomorrow and the fire would

be half as old as she was.

Her grandfather told her the two of them were lucky. It had been just another camping trip in the mountains when the mushroom clouds crowned the final day like seven kings and queens rising to take their smoky crowns all at once. She remembered the first night when it rained ashes. The second night was full of thunderheads vomiting black rain on the mountain. Fish floated to the surface of the stream to look up at the forbidden sky once more with lidless eyes. Corpses of deer and bears littered the forest like sacrifices too heavy and multitudinous to carry to the altars of the new-crowned monarchs of the dark sky. Scavengers flourished. Then the winter came and never left. Arethusa and her grandfather remained. Her parents were in the sky. Her brother was probably in the sky. Now she remained, alone. Arethusa looked up and out from the mouth of the cave. She doubted if she would ever make it to the sky. There were far too many thunderheads for her to reach the heavens where her family waited. Zeus was angry and Hera had died on her own too much.

Arethusa had been warned never to watch the shadows on the cave walls. Even at midday, the meagre sunlight failed to banish the shadow play. But the flames never failed to cast uncertain shapes on the cave walls. Something about the impalpable shadow play pointed towards life. Arethusa closed her eyes and looked and heard:

—I know the shadows remind you of things from before. I remember taking you to your first play in the city, watching movies on that damned big screen television of your father's. I'll never forgive my daughter for him. But this is not for you.

—But it's fun. It's like looking at clouds and finding things. Except these clouds are dark and move faster.

—Yes, but these shadows will take you deeper into the cave. Life is out there, out there beyond the dead trees.

—But I thought it was just us, grandpa?

—For now, it is. But soon it will be just you. If you stay here, it will be just you and the shadows. You'll become a shadow.

—I cast a shadow.

—True. But if you fall into it, you'll never be able to see yourself again.

—You see me.

—That's true, too. But there are others.

—Why don't we go find them, grandpa? Why haven't they come?

—Now is not the time.

—When is the time?

—You'll know. But only if you look that way, out into the pale light.

—It's boring out there.

—It might seem like that now. I'm at sixes and sevens here…gggggg…..kkkkkkkk……gkgkgkgkgkgkgkg….kah…. aaah…

Arethusa shuddered at the thought that her grandfather had presented her with the riddle just to keep her occupied until the shadows took her. Last words were profound words, always. Even his dying concatenation of consonants punctuated by a few merciful vowels could be a clue. The glimmer of cloud to cloud lightning made the cave shimmer for a moment. Specks of quartzite sparkled like jewels geologically tucked away for another Age to hold. Arethusa felt time slipping away. She felt that even the meagre fire would outlive her. The shadows had no beginning or end, just another collection of shapes in flux resembling something or someone. She felt like an old woman waiting to die. Arethusa shivered at the thought and stood up. When she bumped her head, she tried to remember it was herself who had grown and not the cave that was slowly closing its gaping mouth in a slow act of consumption. It had been seven days since she walked out of the cave. Plenty of smoked meat made a girl reluctant to go for a walk in times such as these. Arethusa pulled the bearskin tightly around her wan cheeks. Her eyes braced themselves as she tilted and trudged outward.

Her grandfather's boots were still too big for her but Arethusa had spent half of her life navigating this broken world. Her steps were sure as she wandered in the direction she had never taken. She looked up through the skeletal trees and watched as the clouds exchanged their atmosphere-tearing greetings to one another. The billowing thunderheads of the perpetual cloudscape looked as tumultuous as always. But it smelled like snow. Permafrost crackled beneath her steps like so many shattered skulls shattering again.

—One, two, three, four, five, six, seven....1, 2, 3, 4, 5, 6, 7!

No matter which way she thought of the numbers of her steps, of her breaths, of the dead trees she passed, the numbers were empty and more devoid of meaning than the deadest tree. Even her shout at seven was consumed by the snowscape. If a girl shouted in the forest and nobody was there to hear it, Arethusa knew it made no noise. Riddle solved. But not the riddle that forced her onwards and upwards. Zeus was never far but he was not close. Arethusa had a reckoning with the lingering god of the sky. She demanded something, if only a hint. Woe to anyone or anything, be it god or beast, that dared to stand in the way of such a girl as Arethusa. She nodded in agreement as she continued her ascent.

By the time she reached the end of the skeletal tree line, the wind had obliterated her thoughts. She tasted the snot on her lips and remembered she was mortal. Her wind-tossed equilibrium made the smoked meat digesting in her stomach turn into a pernicious beast clawing its way upwards. Arethusa fell forward and vomited on the frozen rocks. She watched the steam rise and deemed it a suitable offering to the motherfucker above who still played with clouds, that deceitful boy who still called himself king. She laughed at his impotence as not a flake of snow had fallen in the midst of all the fireworks. Arethusa forced herself to swallow and looked up. Six or seven more steps would get her there. If it took eight, she vowed to throw herself off the summit, just another one falling into zero.

When she reached six steps, she saw the divide between herself and the pinnacle of the mountain. There was nothing for her to step onto, just a couple of meters between her sixth step and the seventh. As the wind whipped at her bearskin hood, she leaped forward.

When she came to, she tasted the iron of her blood. The salty life-force was refreshing in the midst of the numbing cold. Her gloved hands felt the sharp hardness of the top of the mountain. Between lightning strikes, her ears rang in accord. Arethusa could still smell snow in spite of her broken nose. She pulled off her left glove and held out her hand. She stared at her ragged palm and waited in half-supplication. She watched as the blood left her hand and her flesh began to resemble the mountain. The lines of her hand were like strata betraying the destiny of so many Ages past and to come. Arethusa did not dare look up, the lightning strikes as inconsequential as the wind. As her field of vision tunneled, she counted down from seven:

—S-seven, six-ix-ix, f-f-f-five, f-four, threeeeee, t-t-t-two, wuh-wuh-nnnn….

It fell into the nexus of her shaking palm. To think of the chances, the infinite parts of the complex machine of causality that led to such a deed made Arethusa laugh softly to herself. She leaned down to her upturned palm and looked. The snowflake looked like it had been born of her own hand. In spite of the wind, it had landed and remained on her freezing flesh. Arethusa's eyes looked into the microcosmic world of each one of the snowflake's points. Crystal worlds within worlds were hinged together in a frozen dance of perfection. The pale light articulated by the lightning was transformed into multifarious atmospheres in the frozen worlds of the snowflake. She stopped thinking and looked and saw. The wind stopped. The lightning ceased. Not another flake fell from the sky. Words were meaningless in the midst of such beauty. Nothing was large or small. There was nothing around. Arethusa held the universe in the palm of her hand. Just a hint of mischief made her count the sides of the universe in spite of her certainty.

—One, two, three, four, five, six…seven!

County Lines

by Hunter McLaren

He hadn't had much, not that much
for him anyway. For his stomach that guzzled bottles
and cups and little plastic shooters. Eyes glazed,
lamps dim, summer tongues, pendulum
hands - ones that pulled me into cat-black nights
where no one could spy. He hadn't had much, but I knew
it was enough for him to stash us away. Enough to make
us ghosts, disappeared persons hanging up coats and hanging
up quilts and closing umbrellas just carefully enough
not to shake all the drops off. Cheeks aglow with apple
whisky, wetter than usual kissing, something like
trying to swallow a swamp, wading for minutes
and minutes and minutes. My mornings began when
I was hung by my shoulders on the clothesline
behind his house that could not be seen from the
road, unfound by neighbors or hovering crows. He
hadn't had much when he said that he wouldn't
hang me up to dry this time. That I wouldn't be
clipped to the line. That I had to evaporate. Drenched and
apologizing. I hadn't had much when I dove into the
cattails across from his front porch, the ones that
went on for miles, the ones that I would break just
to see fly. I armed myself with a net to collect the
shooters and plastic cups that he'd flung into the
grasses, catching them like strange fish, souvenirs
of a drunk who drank to hold me. But I've been him too,
flinging whiskies and embroidering skin, begging men
to throw sheets over themselves. Pretending not
to see them. A barn owl watches me from the tree line,
sees me swimming in cattails and fishing for empties
as the sun ascends over my broke back. The sun
that says to me, *survive it. I know you know how.*

The Sink
by Eric Thralby

There was an old woman made of rags who lived under the sink.
She threatened everybody.
Get your filthy hands off me!
The sink was worse.
He loved cigars. And he was a racist.
He spit at people. He kicked at people.
He was not really a sink but an old man bent to look like a sink who existed over the pipes.
The woman, same, was an old woman who lived under the sink.
The sink liked to cackle and say things suggestive of intercourse.
I bet I make you wet, he'd said. Then he'd spray it in their faces.
The old man did not swallow the contents of their plates.
He spit them onto the floor.

March
by Holly Day

The house groans as the wind tries to rip it apart
tugs at its loose shingles and the ancient tar paper beneath
finds its way through the cracks in the rough window frames
rattles and rustles the plastic taped around the sills.

We groan as we hear the places our house is succumbing
run our hands along the tape that holds the plastic to the
windowsills
worry about the noises in the attic, pray for tiny mice and not
squirrels
or pigeons who have found their way in through some hole not
yet discovered.

Calling Home
by Mickey Collins

phone home
phone home
it's miles away
you're miles away
disconnected
but the landline's still plugged in
by thin wires
and electrical pulses
going this way and that
like memories traversing back and forth
through mountains and oceans in your mind
you almost can't bring-ring yourself to hang on
...
ring-ring
family gathering-ring
parents overbearing-ring
a weight you're shouldering-ring
dangling on a heartstring-ring
splintering-ring
jumping and teetering-ring
erring-ring
regretting
. . .
hello?
hell no
want to hang up
have to hang on
no noose is good noose
you never liked talking on the phone
lips pressed to ears
ears tulips
a rose arise
six feet under
pennies over your eyes
nonsense
no cents
backed up against the wallet
I'm alone again

need a loan again

.

money, honey?
thought you were doney
no, it's not funny
I will always pick up the tab
will always pick up the phone
you can always make a one eighty honey call collect

first, turn around, come collect your life here
everything's dead quiet
it's all gathering-ring dust
I'm gathering-ring dust
your room's just as you left it

your dad went right to work
a quarter past five
and hasn't come back
he's with his girl
feeling alive
fingers up her back
leave it to her beaver
mine's been dammed up
damn kids saw to that
but momma still loves you
in a resentful sort of way
more than deer ole dad
that bucker
what's his excuse
huh?
it's all fawn until soccer games grounding PTA meetings
he may bring-ring the bacon
but someone has to grill it
fry his ass if I ever catch him where he's net supposed to be
serve him with tartar on a bed of court papers
it's 40-15, with no love left
game's over
set's been taken down
the jury's out
but I can't object
can't divorce from the truth
need someone to lie with
someone to come home to

someone to baby me

momma doesn't care about your indiscretions
your life's decisions
she's not mad
I'm not cold
you're just not
who you hot to be

momma had hopes for you
so many plans
but that doesn't matter now
crawl back into the nest
let momma shape you
comb your hair
clean you
bathe you
lick your wounds
your ears
between your toes
momma won't leave you
just love me
don't leave me

it's what you do
when I was due
popped you out into the world
it was my fault really
nine months in the dark isn't enough
wear sunscreen
brighten your teeth
a smile that strikes
listen to your heart
two strikes and out
mind your brain
three strokes and dead
watch your morals
don't get lost in the corals
other fish may flap their fins
other birds may sing so sweet
they'll all try to show you a good time
avoid the murky waters if you branch out
you know mama's nest is the only one you need

near the breast and the rest

mama will preen your feathers and bring-ring you down
pillows to fluff to suffocate to comfort to make a fort
dig a moat but don't forget to draw the bridge
for queen mother, full of grace
will poison your enemies without a trace
she'll clean your laundry of damn spots
your helmet has lost its mettle
watch your head and heed this warning:
beware free room and board
am I boring you?

plant a pea in the bed
place it deep down
in moist fleshy soil
sow what
sew your oats
weave a blanket
cover it, incubate it
splitting an atom
two four eight sixteen
making Adam
stop
abort it
life begins at gestation
poop begins at digestion

I'd like toilet you finish, butt
please don't gripe
don't struggle
don't scream
it's nothing mother hasn't seen
you're looking diaper
white whips will wipe it clean
but you're still full of dirt
dirty behind a dirty mind
flush it down
a royal hot flash
of brown, of yellow
if red please consult a doctor
if it lasts more than four hours
consult a plumber

free your mind of pipe dreams
a brain wash, squeaky clean
spin cycle, nausea
if you can stomach it
no snacks an hour before,
or maybe just a bite
of my warm milk to help you sleep

write your troubles in your dairy
just don't go to bed angry
or cross without praying
or prey without prying
you kneed an answer
but the phone rings-rings through
you get His answering-ring machine

defect from God, You defect
neglect Him as He rejected You
You are made in His image
and mine, too
about fifty-fifty
He's my X, but Y?
You're half mine, but You have all my love
You have His hair, His smile, His nose
momma knows You're perfection
idolized in my eyes
He's just a phoney
God am I lonely

Why don't you phone home more often?
I never hear from you.
I must get off now.
Call on me again.
Home is just a dial tone away.

I'm sorry, the number you are trying to reach has been
disconnected
If you would like to reconnect
kindly go back and try again

Multiple Crucifixes, Hill of Crosses, Lithuania - Roger Camp 97

The Fist

by Bob Selcrosse

The fist climbs into a town. The fist climbs into a canyon. The fist fits inside a cave behind a waterfall.

The boy and the girl were making love in the small lake when the hand came through the waterfall. It was the size of a delivery truck. The waterfall split in two at its wrist and continued streaming down into the pool.

It looked as though it were made of stone, yet obviously was made of flesh. It flexed. It gripped at nothing.

The boy and girl made no sudden movements. The girl was totally still. Her boyfriend moved, as if making to get away very slowly.

The hand snatched him up. It squeezed him.

I love you, he said.

He popped. The hand dropped his corpse, now shaped like a Kleenex, into the water.

He was a cheater, said the hand.

The fist slid back into the waterfall.

BIOS

AJD
AJD has lived and worked in different parts of Oregon for a few decades at many jobs, from assembly line worker to newspaper editor to bookseller.

MAEV BARBA
Dr. Maev Barba attended the Puget Sound Writer's Conference in 2018. She is a PNW native and a great lover of books. She used to sell books door-to-door. A doctor of astronomy, Barba looks into space and considers neither the small as too little, nor the large as too great, for the lover of stars knows there is no limit to dimension.

PHOEBE BLANDING
Phoebe Blanding works at Powell's Books and has a longstanding aversion to making biographical statements.

ROGER CAMP
Roger Camp is the author of three photography books including the award-winning *Butterflies in Flight* (Thames & Hudson, 2002) and *Heat* (Charta, Milano, 2008). His work has appeared in numerous journals including *The New England Review*, *New York Quarterly*, and the *Vassar Review*. He previously worked as a reference librarian at the Santa Ana Public Library and as an analytical bibliographer for the director of the Humanities Research Center at the University of Texas, Austin.

DAN A. CARDOZA
Dan A. Cardoza's fiction, nonfiction, and poetry have met international acceptance. Most recently his work has been featured in *Five-Two Crime Poetry*, *Black Petal*, *Cabinet of Heed*, *Cleaver*, *Danse Macabre*, *Dissections*, *Entropy*, *Gravel*, *Liquid Imagination*, *Montana Mouthful*, *New Flash Fiction Review*, *Rabid Oak* and *Spelk*.

JOHN CHROSTEK
John Chrostek is a Pushcart-nominated poet, playwright and author who works at Powell's City of Books in Portland, OR. His work has been featured in publications such as *Artemis*, *River Heron Review*, and *Cathexis Press*.

MICKEY COLLINS
~~Mickey rights wrongs. Mickey wrongs rites.~~ Mickey writes words, sometimes wrong words but he tries to get it write.

Ben Crowley

Ben Crowley is from Pittsburgh, Pennsylvania. He is happy to get back to writing because he has already paid a kidney to *Deep Overstock* and is considering dishing out a finger and thumb. Ben used to sort books for the Amazon warehouse, in our beautiful backcountry of western Pittsburgh. Now he drives a truck, but he's still selling books at whatever diner, truckstop or seedy hotel he finds himself in.

Jacob Davis

Jacob Davis resides in Salem, Oregon, where he works as a bookseller at the Book Bin. He graduated from Portland State University with an English Major and lives a relatively quiet life with his wife.

Holly Day

Holly Day's poetry has recently appeared in *Asimov's Science Fiction*, *Grain*, and *Harvard Review*. Her newest poetry collections are *In This Place, She Is Her Own* (Vegetarian Alcoholic Press), *A Wall to Protect Your Eyes* (Pski's Porch Publishing), *Folios of Dried Flowers and Pressed Birds* (Cyberwit. net), *Where We Went Wrong* (Clare Songbirds Publishing), *Into the Cracks* (Golden Antelope Press), and *Cross Referencing a Book of Summer* (Silver Bow Publishing), while her newest nonfiction books are *Music Theory for Dummies* and *Tattoo FAQ*.

Amanda Depperschmidt

Amanda Depperschmidt is a bookseller in the PPR zone at Powell's City of Books. Her writing focuses on archival theory, climate destruction, and animals.

S.C. Downey

S.C. is a bookseller at Powell's City of Books in Portland and a dedicated lifelong learner. She believes in serendipitous moments leading people to books that can alter their life. She is honored to facilitate those connections or maybe just help make someone's day a little brighter. Inspired by so many others, she enjoys sharing through creative expression in images, writing and spoken word.

Robert Eversmann

Robert Eversmann works for Deep Overstock. His website is roberteversmann.com

L. Fid

L. Fid is a member of a pseudonymous arts collective dedicated to world domination.

Mark Hurtubise

During the 1970s, numerous pieces were accepted for publication. Then family, teaching, two college presidencies and for 12 years president of an Inland Northwest community foundation. After a four decade hiatus, he is now attempting to outpace a tortoise. Within the past two and half years, his works have appeared in *Apricity Magazine* (Texas), *Adelaide Literary Magazine, twice* (New York), *Bones Journal* (Denmark), *Modern Haiku* (Rhode Island), *Ink In Thirds* (Alabama), *Atlas Poetica* (Maryland), *Burningword Literary Journal* (Indiana), *The Spokesman-Review* (Washington), *Frogpond Journal* (New York), *Stanford Social Innovation Review* (California) and *Alliance* (United Kingdom).

Ariel Kusby

Ariel Kusby is a writer and bookseller based in Portland, Oregon. She currently works in the Rose and Orange rooms at Powell's City of Books, where she pays special attention to children's books about witches, odd cookbooks, and gnome gardening guides. You can check out her writing at www.arielkusby.com.

Ari Mathae

Ari Mathae is a bookseller, editor, and podcast producer based in Portland. They graduated from Portland State University with their master's degree in Book Publishing.

Caroline McCulloch

Caroline McCulloch is a former Powell's bookseller who works in publishing. When she's not reading, she's exploring Portland or hanging out with her one-eyed cat, Pluto.

Hunter McLaren

Hunter McLaren is a college graduate from Central Michigan University with a Bachelor of Science in English Language, Literature, and Writing. He also has a creative writing certificate and a minor in Ethics, Value, and Society. He is an emerging poet with eight pieces published, passionately seeking more publication opportunities. He proclaims the goal of his work is to unseat comfort and confront surreal or traumatic themes in creative and cathartic ways.

Azalea Micketti

Azalea is a writer, director, actor, and bookseller living in the weirdest place on earth (open for heated discussion). She loves words, knows a little too much about Shakespeare, and will happily discuss books for literal hours.

HAYDEN MOORE

Hayden Moore was born and raised in Georgia and has lived in New York City for the past twelve years. In the past six months, he has been published three times for his short stories: twice in *Corner Bar Magazine*, once in *Metonym Literary Journal*. He lives with his wife and cat on the waters of Jamaica Bay in Queens.

LEANNA MOXLEY

Leanna Moxley spends most of her time wandering in and out of fictional dimensions, often guiding others through these portals in her work as a Powell's bookseller, and sometimes as a college writing teacher.

ELIZABETH NEAL

Elizabeth Neal is a Portland actress and bookseller. She is proud of her Union, ILWU Local 5.

TIMOTHY ARLISS O'BRIEN

Timothy Arliss O'Brien is an interdisciplinary artist in music composition, writing, and visual arts. His goal is to connect people to accessible new music that showcases virtuosic abilities without losing touch of authentic emotions. He has premiered music with The Astoria Music Festival, Cascadia Composers, Sound of Late's 48 hour Composition Competition and ENAensemble's Serial Opera Project. He also wants to produce writing that connects the reader to themselves in a way that promotes wonder and self realization. He has published several novels (*Dear God I'm a Faggot, They*), and has written for Look Up Records (Seattle), Our Bible App, and *Deep Overstock*: The Bookseller's Journal. He has also combined his passion for poetry with his love of publishing and curates the podcast The Poet Heroic. Check out more of his writing, and his full discography at his website: www.timothyarlissobrien.com

BOB SELCROSSE

Bob Selcrosse grew up with his mother, selling books, in the Pacific Northwest. He is now working on a book about a book. It is based in the Pacific Northwest. The book is *The Cabinet of Children*.

KYA STARLING

Kya Starling is an editor who lives in Vancouver, BC.

SABRINA STEIN

Sabrina works at the butt of consumerism in a wonderful bookstore (Powell's), where she loves to touch books, read humans and drink ungodly hot coffee.

Eric Thralby

Captain by trade, Cpt. Eric Thralby works wood in his long off-days. He time-to-time pilots the Bremerton Ferry (Bremerton—Vashon; Vahon—Bremerton), while other times sells books on amazon.com, SellerID: plainpages. He'll sell any books the people love, strolling down to library and yard sales, but he loves especially books of Romantic fiction, not of risqué gargoyles, not harlequin romance, but knights, errant or of the Table. Eric has not published before, but has read in local readings at the Gig Harbor Candy Company and the Lavender Inne, also in Gig Harbor.

ZB Wagman

ZB Wagman is a writer based in Portland, Oregon. When not writing, he spends his days working at the Beaverton City Library.

Peter Waldor

Peter Waldor is the author of *Door to a Noisy Room* (Alice James Books), *The Wilderness Poetry of Wu Xing* (Pinyon Publishing), *Who Touches Everything* (Settlement House), which won the National Jewish Book Award, *The Unattended Harp* (Settlement House), *State of the Union* (Kelsay Books) and *Gate Posts with No Gate* (Shanti Arts). Waldor was the Poet Laureate of San Miguel County, Colorado from 2014 to 2015. His work has appeared in many journals, including the *American Poetry Review*, *Ploughshares*, the *Iowa Review*, the *Colorado Review*, *Poetry Daily*, *Verse Daily* and *Mothering Magazine*. Waldor lives in Trout Lake, Colorado.

Sarah Wei

Sarah Wei is a poet and writer of children's literature. When she is not meditating on the Meaning of Life, you can find her in the kitchen, wrestling a lump of bread dough into submission. This is not a metaphor. Or maybe it is.

Nicholas Yandell

Nicholas Yandell is a composer, who sometimes creates with words instead of sound. In those cases, he usually ends up with fiction and occasionally poetry. He also paints and draws, and often all these activities become combined, because they're really not all that different from each other, and it's all just art right?
When not working on creative projects, Nick works as a bookseller at Powell's Books in Portland, Oregon, where he enjoys being surrounded by a wealth of knowledge, as well as working and interacting with creatively stimulating people. He has a website where he displays his creations; it's nicholasyandell.com. Check it out!